BEGGARS CAN BE CHOSEN

An Inspirational Journey Through The Invitations of Jesus

By Chris Maxwell

Copyright © 2003 by Chris Maxwell

Beggars Can Be Chosen
by Chris Maxwell

Printed in the United States of America
Library of Congress Control Number: 2003091676
ISBN 591605-76-8

All rights reserved. No part of this publication may be reproduced or transmitted in any form or by any means without written permission of the publisher.

Unless otherwise indicated, Scripture is taken from the Holy Bible, New International Version, NIV, Copyright ©1973, 1978, 1984 by International Bible Society, Zondervan. All rights reserved.

Xulon Press
www.XulonPress.com

Xulon Press books are available in bookstores everywhere, and on the Web at www.XulonPress.com.

Chapter 6, A Friend to the Friendless originally appeared in the article "Pharisee in the Mirror," in *Charisma,* April 1999.

Chapter 8, Coming to Christ for the Rest of Your Life originally appeared in *Today's Pentecostal Evangel,* May 28, 2000.

Chapter 9, Thirsty for Love, originally appeared in the article "Out Where the Sinners Are," in *Charisma,* August, 1998.

Chapter 18, Spending the Night, originally appeared on the website: http://artisanitorium.thehydden.com/fiction/maxwell/spendingnight.htm, February, 2003.

Several portions of these chapters have been included in Chris Maxwell's e-mail devotional, called "Another Day Along the Way." Those wishing to be added to that list can contact Chris at CMaxMan@aol.com.

TABLE OF CONTENTS

Foreword vii
Preface xi
Introduction—The Invitations of Jesus 15
Chapter 1—Simple Invitation 19
Chapter 2—Following the Leader 31
Chapter 3—Gone Fishin' 41
Chapter 4—Excuses, Excuses 51
Chapter 5—A Familiar Face in a Frightening Place 59
Chapter 6—A Friend to the Friendless 69
Chapter 7—Life After Death 81
Chapter 8—Coming to Christ for the Rest of Your Life 91
Chapter 9—Thirsty for Love 99
Chapter 10—Missing the Boat 107
Chapter 11—Awards, Autographs and a Kid in The Middle . 117
Chapter 12—Leaving The Back Door Open 125
Chapter 13—No Sudden Moves, Please 135
Chapter 14—Beggars Can Be Chosen 145
Chapter 15—A Small Man With A Tall Plan 155
Chapter 16—Dressed For Success 165
Chapter 17—Does Anybody Really Know What Time It Is? . 175

Chapter 18—Spending the Night 185
Chapter 19—Make Reservations: How to Wake Up in a
    Wonderful Place............................... 193
Chapter 20—Come and Have Breakfast................ 201
Conclusion— Jesus of the Invitations 211
Notes.. 215

FOREWORD

In late 2002 I boarded a plane bound for Atlanta from Orlando. After greeting the flight attendant I silently prayed, as I usually do on airplanes, "Lord, please arrange my seat assignment." I have been known to share my faith during flights, and I always try to make myself available to talk to those who end up sitting next to me. On this particular morning, God had a special appointment for me. His name was Jason.

When I saw him coming down the aisle toward my seat, I secretly hoped his boarding assignment was for 32F, right next to me. He looked unsure of himself, perhaps because the disapproving stares coming from other passengers were so obvious. Jason was a Goth. He was dressed in black pants, a black shirt with black netting over it, and tall black boots that laced all the way up to his knees. He sported several earrings, a metal stud in his chin and a heavy-metal dog collar with spikes.

When he arrived at my row, the chains attached to his pants clinked and clanged against the seat. He grunted as if to apologize for being seated next to me. I hopped up and greeted him, to his surprise.

"You must be sitting here. What's your name," I asked.

As we taxied toward the runway, I learned Jason's sad story. He was 21, and his parents were divorced when he was 13. He was traveling to see his dad in Las Vegas, and dreading the visit because he knew his father would not like his Gothic attire. He fidgeted nervously with his bracelets, all the while complaining about how long it took for him to take off his boots during the airport security check.

After the plane took off, I told him I liked his ornate rings, some of which were fashioned to look like the claws of cats or the talons of hawks. He told me about each one, since they were all given to him by other Goth friends. Although they might look scary to some people, the rings actually had sentimental value to Jason. They represented his isolated world, a world he had entered in order to protect himself from the pain in his dysfunctional family.

"Ever heard of The Kitchen in Miami?" I asked. Jason couldn't believe that I knew anything about an obscure Goth nightclub in South Florida, since I certainly didn't look like a Goth. I explained that I worked for a Christian magazine, and that we had done a story on Goths and what they believe. He seemed genuinely surprised—and intrigued by my knowledge of his subculture.

"Did you know that there are some Goths who are Christians?" I asked. He had never heard of that, so I explained that knowing Jesus Christ has nothing to do with what kind of clothes you wear. Christians, I reminded him, are Christians because they love Jesus, not because they wear conservative suits or church clothes.

I then realized that Jason had never met a Christian who had not judged him for his appearance. God put me in 32G on that plane that day just so this young man could know that the Father loves him.

For the next hour I showed a genuine interest in Jason's music, his friends and his drawings, which he pulled out of his backpack halfway to Atlanta. I steered the conversation to the subject of his dad, and, as I expected, that hit a nerve. Then I reminded him that His heavenly Father would never reject him because of what he wore or who he associated with. By the time we reached Atlanta, Jason took my business card and said he would ask his mother to call me. She had already tried to commit suicide once.

I have never talked to Jason since that day in October 2002, but I know that God used me that morning to issue an invitation. I didn't

Foreword

pray with him to become a Christian—someone else will have that opportunity later. I simply sowed a seed, and demonstrated to a lost son that Jesus is looking for him.

That is what evangelism is all about—not scoring points or following a script, but participating in Jesus' grand scheme to recover people who have lost their way in a dark world. And when Jesus directs our evangelism, it becomes an adventure that will leave you breathless.

This book is about that kind of adventurous evangelism. The author, Chris Maxwell, is a dear friend of mine who cares for lost people more than anyone I know. He has been infected with a passion for genuine, Spirit-led evangelism for years. I pray this book will help spread that passion.

—J. Lee Grady

PREFACE

B*eggars Can Be Chosen*" was conceived in a time of inner turmoil emerging from a hope to see more lasting change in my life and in the lives of those I share life with. All ministers long to see a greater response, and all exist close to a nagging pain caused by seeing so many people resisting the word that can help them most.

Conceived in the context of that concern, the birth of this book came in the room of prayer. These meditations came to life for me not in trite, cliché-ridden prayer. They came in a time of squarely facing myself, my ministry and my hope for much more.

I knelt in prayer desperately longing for direction. I wanted to see souls saved and lives radically altered, but I did not see it happening. I knew not whether I was missing its occurrence, if my assessment was faulty or if I merely longed for the wrong proof. Whatever the facts, my frustration melted into inspiration as direction came. Gimmicks and games would not reach the lost. The best method would be the Jesus method. So I plunged into a study that produced this series of sermons examining how Christ "evangelized" the people of His day. If adapted to our times, the timeless principles would surely work. Little did I know the profound impact these stories would have upon me.

A subject of this type could easily lend itself to ventures down many side streets. I have avoided some while traveling others. In attempting to remain faithful to the biblical text, any work of this sort will nevertheless reveal personal bias, and some of my own hidden prejudices will undoubtedly emerge. I must confess, however, that I have been challenged and changed by this study as some of my most tightly held assumptions have been gloriously shattered.

This book is not a theological examination of such topics as foreknowledge, predestination or the sovereignty of God, though such truths obviously relate to the subject matter and are woven throughout. This is also not a subtle attempt at accepting or rejecting the controversial "Lordship Salvation" issue that has been recently swirling through evangelicalism, but I do not fail to notice conditions or expectations Christ appears to place on certain potential followers. By trying to zero in exclusively on the narratives, I do not mention important subjects like baptism and church membership. The collection is not a running exegetical commentary on the various texts, nor is it exhaustive. I have omitted stories that could have been included; I have included some that others may have chosen to omit.

In these pages I seek to assist us in entering the narratives—answering some questions and raising others—in hopes that by hearing Christ invite people to Himself we can:

(1) hear Christ inviting us, and
(2) better understand how He would have us invite others to Him.

My prayer is that by entering these stories we will allow Jesus to challenge our customs and clichés, enabling us to forge a new, more biblical evangelistic direction.

My family and friends know I try, but fail, to regularly succeed in living out these principles. But, I thank God for them. Debbie, Taylor, Aaron and Graham are wonderful blessings from my Heavenly Father. I also thank God for my parents who raised me to believe in God, for my terrific sisters and their families, for my in-laws, and for other relatives who care so much. Mama died too soon for me, but I still seek to imitate her.

Preface

My church family has truly lived as a church: sinners saved by grace, who depend on God to help us live out His calling. Their love and acceptance is first class. They cared for me before and after my battle with an illness that changed my life, my style, my schedule. A few men mentored me directly. Many men and women have indirectly. I have listed books to read, but so many books and songs and articles have displayed more than literary ability; they have reflected truth and grace. I thank my accountability group for helping me live life even when the weather is partly cloudy (they will get the joke). The editors (Dianne Chambers, Mary DeMent, Fran Long, Doree Rice, Jim Rovira, and Paul Smith) who took my wild, poetic rambling and transformed it into readable work deserve a huge thanks. And, I thank God for my doctors and nurses. He used you to save my life. I'm praying I will always be used to save the souls of many.

Will *Beggars Can Be Chosen* help me, help us do that?

Our calendars, our history and our holidays reveal the impact Christ had on planet earth. That impact has only intensified through the centuries because of the ones who accepted His Invitation. When He walked the dusty roads of Galilee He invited the good, the bad and the ugly to follow Him. He chose many to be on His team; some accepted, others rejected His Invitation.

He continues to invite. May God assist us in learning more about Jesus' Invitation to us through these ancient dramas. These stories, as well as the continuing work of God's Spirit, prove clearly that beggars can be chosen. That, my friend, is great news!

Chris Maxwell

Introduction

THE INVITATIONS OF JESUS

A group of eager youngsters converge on a playground for an after-school game of baseball. Chuck, the tallest, is in charge. He carries the only bat and ball among them as symbols of his supremacy. Chatting nervously, the other boys jockey for conversation with, or a place close to, their tribal leader. Though young, the players know well how hostile life can be when popularity and acceptance are at stake.

The competitors ready themselves with warm-up tosses and exaggerated challenges. Chuck summons the group after brief moments of preparation, informing them that he and Wilson, as usual, are the captains who will choose teams. The group has endured the process frequently. The talented, or the most popular, get picked first. The awkward hopefuls experience the humiliation of being chosen last. If at all. That's how it is for Allen.

He is overweight and uncoordinated. His thick glasses and hand-me-down clothes provide ample ammunition for taunting from the insecure peers who never ignore such a perfect target. His name is Allen. Rarely do the boys call him Allen, opting instead for jests that attack his weight, his eyesight, his clothing or his clumsiness. So, on this day, he expects the usual round of ridicule as he suffers through the endless few minutes of rejection. Allen, aware of his limitations, desperately longs for an opportunity, for a chance, for a friend.

Chuck chooses first. He always does. The eager candidates can easily predict the order of selection. Chuck regularly orchestrates the process to guarantee himself the upper hand. And to insure that Wilson gets stuck with Allen.

Today, however, is different. Chuck looks relaxed. He doesn't hurry. He looks over the group several times, smiling as if he knows something they do not. Then, he shocks them all. He picks Allen. He picks Allen first. Not a good hitter, a good pitcher, or a good comedian. Allen. As other boys snicker, Chuck says, "I'm serious." Then he says, "Come on, Allen, I want you on my team."

Allen initially thinks he is the victim of another cruel joke. But Chuck is serious, and gives Allen a feeling of exhilaration he has long awaited. Someone wants him. Today, at least for today, he is not the cursed, but the chosen.

Allen proudly stands beside Chuck in that place all the boys desire. Chuck hands Allen the bat and says, "You lead off."

Oh, the beauty of fairy tales. Underdogs win. Frogs become princes.

The story of our after-school ballplayers may not happen in our neighborhoods, but we would love for it to. Hearts leap when reading of the friendless finding a friend, of the rejected receiving acceptance. While we convince ourselves it can't come true in real life, such scenarios make for pleasant dreams and engaging stories.

But what about real life? Are we correct in insisting that the weak can never become strong or the obscure great? Maybe we hope these lofty plots will play out in life because we, like Allen, feel useless and awkward. If fairy tales do come true we want a shot at the lead role. We long to be chosen, to be wanted. Yet, all too often, we walk home unwanted while we hear others playing in the distance.

In the Gospels of Grace, we catch a glimpse of our dreams of glory. We see that fairy tales can come true. Jesus, this historical World Shaker, claimed to espouse as His mission the releasing of the imprisoned and the loving of the unloved. He walked into the

Introduction

playground of the ancient eastern world and chose players for His team. His choices shocked those chosen, and baffled those observing on the stands of tradition and political correctness.

The gospel teaches, in a sense, that He has drafted each of us. Though we stand back, awkward and amazed, He hands us the bat. Though frogs, He kisses us. Though ugly stepchildren, He makes the slipper somehow fit.

He came, and comes, to give life to the lifeless.

The stories that follow force us to face facts of His coming and His inviting. Examine the narratives from which come the Invitations of Jesus. Listen as He invited. Listen as He invites. Let the events fill your mind. Let the beauty warm your heart.

Respond to His call. Let the dreams become true in you as did many of the characters who heard Him two thousand years ago when He spoke the words, "Come, follow me." He awaits a reply.

Chapter 1

A SIMPLE INVITATION

The next day John was there again with two of his disciples. When he saw Jesus passing by, he said, "Look, the Lamb of God!"

When the two disciples heard him say this, they followed Jesus. Turning around, Jesus saw them following and asked, "What do you want?"

They said, "Rabbi" (which means Teacher), "where are you staying?"

"Come," he replied, "and you will see."

So they went and saw where he was staying, and spent that day with him. It was about the tenth hour.

Andrew, Simon Peter's brother, was one of the two who heard what John had said and who had followed Jesus. The first thing Andrew did was to find his brother Simon and tell him, "We have found the Messiah" (that is, the Christ). And he brought him to Jesus.

Jesus looked at him and said, "You are Simon son of John. You will be called Cephas" (which, when translated, is Peter).[1]

—St. John

> Men were to be His method of winning the world to God.[2]
>
> —*Robert E. Coleman*

> We are constantly on a stretch, if not a strain, to devise new methods, new plans, new organizations to advance the church and secure enlargement and efficiency for the gospel. This trend of the day has a tendency to lose sight of the man or sink the man in the plan or organization. God's plan is to make much of the man, far more of him than of anything else. Men are God's method. The Church is looking for better methods; God is looking for better men.[3]
>
> —*E. M. Bounds*

In sports, journalists often ask team owners or coaches to name players around which they would most like to assemble a franchise. Young superstars open eyes. The question is not, "Who is the most talented individual?," but "What player would be the best foundation on which to construct a championship team?"

Scott Herring, Assistant General Manager of the Orlando Magic, describes the non-stop scheme of designing a team. He says, "As we consider free agents and draft picks, we look for more than what most people can see. They need to excel as a player, but they also must play with the team. Do they fit with multiple parts? Are they leaders or followers? What happens in their personal lives? Look at successful teams and you will see how one piece can complete a puzzle. That piece does it not just on the court, though. Their attitudes must set up team harmony for the goal of winning. It can't be just a 'me first' mindset."

Such executives love to dream of taking their players of choice and racing them toward a first place finish. Draft order, salary caps, contract disputes and injuries wake visionaries from their wishes. Few obtain the players of their dreams. They settle for doing their best to amass a team of players which forms a complete puzzle, complementing each other and working in harmony toward the goal of winning.

How did Jesus pick His team?

As Christ emerged from the wilderness to begin His public ministry, He faced a monumental task. On a far more vital plane than that of piecing together a championship team, Christ faced a season of choices. His decisions would shape the future of a planet. They would affect life beyond time. Who would He choose for His team? How could He assemble a small group, enroll them in a three-year, personal-training plan for the purpose of perpetuating His love story around the world and across the years?

Though by today's standards the world at that time was sparsely populated, the land of Christ overflowed with people. He had many options for players. He could have chosen priests, merchants, laborers, shrewd business leaders, philosophers, governmental officials, paupers. Maybe a prostitute or a politician. Maybe a marketing expert for promotion or a corporate consultant for financial success. Like today, society contained a wide array of possibilities.

Jesus began His ministry making those choices, piecing together His team. He revealed much about Himself and His dream by the players of choice. Illustrating the political arena, Gayle Erwin put it in perspective:

> "When we get a new president in the United States, everyone watches to see who he surrounds himself with—what kind of staff and cabinet he chooses. So the Son of God comes to earth and begins to reveal what kind of 'reign' he will have by putting together his traveling band."[4]

Christ began choosing His cabinet without the international scrutiny that surrounds presidential appointments or the media hype that frames NBA drafts. In relative obscurity, Jesus of Nazareth extended simple Invitations to select people. Those would join Him in Inviting the world to link with them. The simplicity of its inception offers little clue to the way individuals and nations would be shaken by the grand scheme of this Carpenter's Kid.

Our scene began with the spotlight on a rather odd character. John was Christ's first cousin. He was also an unrestrained, discourteous, outdoor preacher wearing bargain basement rejects and living on a diet more befitting an animal. John baptized people as they acknowledged their sinfulness, and had reluctantly baptized Jesus in the Jordan River. God's Spirit revealed to John that his cousin was the Messiah Israel had awaited for centuries. But the thrill of being related to the Savior of the world had a downside; the rise of Christ's ministry would result in the dismantling of John's.

Beautifully, though, John avoided being drawn into a power play. Instead of pouting, he pointed the way to Jesus. He could resist his destiny as a set-up man, but he graciously encouraged his entourage to leave and join with Jesus. Two of his disciples, Andrew and one presumed to be John, the author of the gospel account, followed a Man the baptizer called "The Lamb of God."

INTEREST

Why the interest? What caused those two men to so willingly accept roles on Christ's inexperienced team? Probably not the looks of Jesus. Or His voice or His vocabulary or His endorsements. I doubt Jesus was a handsome hunk who naturally drew men and women with a Hollywood persona. "He had no beauty of majesty to attract us to him, nothing in his appearance that we should desire him,"[5] wrote the poet/prophet Isaiah 700 years before young Mary wrapped the baby Jesus in "cloths and placed him in a manger."[6]

What was it? Two things:

1. The witness of John
2. Their zeal to find the truth

John and Andrew had grown to trust John the baptizer. They had seen sincerity at the root of his eccentric ways. By following him eagerly, by observing him regularly, they developed an awareness of John's drive to enter and proclaim God's Kingdom. The witness of John the baptizer gave ample reason for the two to continue their pursuit of reality by pursuing Jesus. Like us, they were more ready to accept advice from someone they trusted. They knew John. They knew his passion for right. When he spoke, they listened.

The two were seekers. Aligning themselves with the controversial baptizer proves they possessed deep desires for reality. Before a person can fully agree to the pronouncement that "Jesus is the answer," the person must begin asking the questions to which this world has no answers. "He who seeks, finds."[7]

Finding truth is a grace. But the gift falls into the lap of those who look for it, who long for it. Since a disciple is the one who, by definition, has accepted the role of a pupil, the fact that John and Andrew submitted themselves to learning under John the baptizer indicated an openness to truth and a willingness to sit at the feet of one believed to possess that truth. From their perspective, following Jesus was the next step in their progressive pursuit of truth. "They were filled with questions and they needed answers. They possess no plan, they simply stood before him on the threshold of hope."[8]

Jesus noticed their interest. He asked them, "What do you want?" Addressing Him as Teacher, they answered with a question of their own, "Where are you staying?"

Their inquiry sounded like that of a child asking permission to stay up late or like the whimpers of a pet longing to sleep inside sheltered from the cold. "In their awkward way they were asking if they could tag along with him."[9]

Are we seeking to notice life's deep, nagging questions? Are we willing to answer life's deep and nagging questions? Are we willing to admit we're often missing the answers ourselves? Do we possess the hunger Andrew and John exemplified? Are we humble enough to ask permission to tag along? As I look back over my life, I am moved by the memories of people that discipled me. By allowing me to "tag along," they pointed me to the Lamb of God. I think of:

- A mother whose smile radiated God's love and whose life reflected real Christianity.
- An older cousin who always had time for me. He taught me how to hit a fastball and shoot a jump shot, but upon his conversion he began to teach me about eternal things.

- A high school teacher who accepted me as I was, but who challenged me to go all the way for God. Through his life and words I gained an understanding of the Third Person of the Trinity.
- A college professor who taught me more than Greek and Homiletics; he taught me about prayer and people. I consider him my mentor.

Most of us want to be teachers rather than students. We enjoy thinking we know all the answers, that we see the complete picture. Fortunately, in our story, John's pupils didn't. They hungered for more. They didn't hide the hunger beneath layers of religion, assertiveness or false courtesy.

Before another person can significantly impact our lives we must let them know our interest. "Where are you staying?," asked the seekers. They didn't know the ramifications of that question.

INVITATION

Christ's Invitation followed their interest: "Come and you will see." Jesus opened His arms, His home, His life to the seekers. "Come"—the central theme of this study and all of Scripture—opened entrance into a new world for those two men. The Inviter invited them behind the scenes of history's most remarkable drama.

The word "come" is common in the Bible. Strong's Concordance uses 17 columns to list the references. In this study's text, the word is a present imperative, indicating a "command to do something in the future which involves continuous or repeated action."[10] Christ invited them over for lunch. But He wanted more. He wanted them to join Him for life. So we see the beauty of the gospel beginning to take shape:

> "It is like a fairy story—the reigning monarch adopts waifs and strays to make princes of them—but, praise God, it is not a fairy story: it is hard and solid fact, founded on the bedrock of free and sovereign grace."[11]

A Simple Invitation

In choosing His followers, Christ purposed "that they be with him."[12] Few people would turn down an invitation to visit a famous star one-on-one. Multitudes, however, daily reject an Invitation from the King of the Universe to "come and see." If Jesus physically appeared and bid us to sit with Him, wouldn't we accept that intriguing offer? Why do we refuse when the Host is invisible?

He wanted to be with Andrew and John. He wants to be with us. Personally. He longs for humans to fellowship with Him. Until we do, we will aimlessly float from one attempt at gratification to another, hoping to satisfy a deep, inner longing only Christ can satiate.

"The great hallmark of men and women of God throughout the ages has been their close walk and intimacy with God."[13] It is to such an experience that Christ invited John and Andrew. Throughout Scripture, biblical writers highlighted that truth. The gospels speak of "abiding in Christ." The epistles refer to "walking in the Spirit" and to living "in Christ." That latter phrase appears to be the apostle Paul's favorite; to him, successful individual and community living depended completely on one's relationship with Jesus.

John and Andrew were invited to Jesus. By Jesus. He invited "them to come and gain from Him an insight into the mind and purpose of God" and begin understanding that "discipleship means nothing less than abiding with Him forever."[14]

INSTRUCTION

Subsequent to the interest of Andrew and John, and the Invitation of Jesus, a third action occurred. Jesus immediately began the never-ending task of educating His new companies. They joined Him at 4:00 PM. They stayed with Him the remainder of the day. Where does the Bible say He taught them? Where is a list of truths He tried to drill into them?

The Bible mentions nothing about His teaching in this narrative. That is precisely the point. Just as the Invitation comes on the heels of their interest, the instruction begins when they respond to the

Invitation. Convinced that truth is more caught than taught, Jesus opened His life to His followers. "Having called his men, Jesus made it a point to be with them. This was the essence of his training program—just letting the disciples follow him."[15]

Jesus didn't stop with "Do as I say." By sharing His life, He said, "Do as I do." He displayed on-the-job training. The three-year seminary degree He offered His initial students can only be earned in active involvement. His method of instruction remains the same today. More schools, businesses and ministries appear to be moving in that direction, but Christ's lesson plans look different from modern educational techniques.

> "We have brought students away from life into a classroom. Jesus drew students into the middle of life. We have limited the time for education to an hour or two. Jesus gave all his time to educating his disciples. We have glorified in ever-larger classes. Jesus chose twelve to be 'with him'. We have kept teachers in isolated non-revealing lecture roles. Jesus exposed his life to the disciples. We dump our children into a reservoir of bodies and leave the training to strangers. The Bible gives the first responsibility to the parents."[16]

The Old Testament examples of Moses and Joshua, Elijah and Elisha. Paul and Timothy in the New Testament. They illustrate the principle of education through personal discipleship. Life's laboratory: that's the believers' classroom. The popularity of such an approach is on the upswing. Non-traditional learning-on-the-job programs must blend with classroom depth, wedding education with occupation. It works. The route allows participants to recognize the value of learning by, and while, doing.

The call to a life of learning went out from Christ to the initial disciples. He likewise invites us to a life of intimate learning. He longs to be with us. Responding to His Invitation propels the believer into a new existence. Radical changes begin to emerge from the closeness between Teacher and pupil. Notice a few of the life altering truths that the pupils of Christ will grow into:

C— Comfort...To a world troubled with stress, Jesus gives comfort.[17]
H— Hope...To a world in despair, Jesus gives hope. [18]
R— Reality...To a world drunk on a lie, Jesus gives reality.[19]
I— Innocence...To a world burdened by guilt, Jesus gives innocence.[20]
S— Security...To a world bound by insecurity, Jesus gives security.[21]
T— Triumph...To a world in depression, Jesus gives triumph.[22]

INFLUENCE

The success of educational efforts is proven, not by test scores but by practical application. Basing our evaluation on that premise, we determine that Christ's beginning efforts succeeded. He didn't quiz the followers or pressure them to do or say something impressive. They responded naturally. Their efforts to influence others with their newfound Truth grew out of their time with the Teacher. Though their time in His classroom had been brief, the impact began an eternal change in their lives.

Andrew raced to Simon bearing the good news: The Messiah had arrived! He welcomed them! Having been influenced by Christ, Andrew, in turn, influenced others. That serves as the blueprint for propagating the gospel. Then for them. Now for us. Those influenced must influence.

> "It is the nature of Christian experience that those who enjoy it, however partially, desire to share it with others. It is not therefore surprising that, as soon as the day dawns, the first thing Andrew does is to find his brother Simon, break the news to him that Christ had appeared, and bring him to Jesus."[23]

Notice the progression of Andrew's influence:

1. He found Simon.
2. He told Simon.
3. He took Simon to Jesus.
4. Jesus renamed Simon.

Andrew, so moved by the One John pointed Him toward, could not keep the experience to himself. Like the early church Luke would write about years later, Andrew could not help but speak of the things he had seen and heard.[24] He discovered a cure for the disease plaguing the human race. The cure demanded distribution.

Where would he begin? The old saying claims "charity begins at home." Here we see such home-centered love in action. Andrew took the message to his brother Simon: an arrogant, hard-working fisherman we will learn more about later. Andrew did his part by finding him, telling him and taking him to Jesus. The Master took it from there.

So we see the plan of Christ at work even at the early stage of His ministry. He knew that "one cannot transform a world except as individuals in the world are transformed, and individuals cannot be transformed except as they are molded in the hands of the Master."[25]

Remembering our dual goal in this study—to hear Christ invite us and to learn how to invite others to Him—this initial narrative offers valuable insights. Interest. Invitation. Instruction. Influence. "Jesus did not use manipulation or intimidation as a recruiting method."[26] Neither does He use those tactics to Invite us. Should we follow His example and refuse such methods to influence others?

But influence them we must. The story informs me of what I should do. Will I? Here is my list.

Be a seeker, expressing desperate interest in the One believed to be the Truth. Listen for, and respond to, His compassionate Invitation. Slow from the rush of routine. Enter the classroom of the Great Instructor. Remain at His feet. Allow the overflow of that education to spill into home, neighborhood, job and leisure.

If I live it, if you live it, how many Andrews and Simons will enjoy our influence?

A Simple Invitation

REJOICE that this ministry helps share the Invitation: Chuck Colson's personal prison experience and his frequent visits to prisons prompted new concerns about the efficacy of the American criminal justice system and made him one of the nation's influential voices for criminal justice reform. Colson's recommendations have brought together legislators from both political parties and divergent philosophical viewpoints. In 1983, Colson established Justice Fellowship®, a faith-based criminal justice reform group. To help stem the cycle of crime and poverty, Prison Fellowship, under Colson's leadership, introduced Angel Tree®, a program that provides Christmas presents to more than 500,000 children of inmates annually on behalf of their incarcerated parents. These simple acts of kindness have revitalized hope and reconciliation among millions of children and their families, many of whom subsist below the poverty level. Angel Tree has also launched a summer camping program, partnering with churches around the country to send the children of prisoners to a Christian summer camp. www.pfm.org

RELEASE your worries by praying, "God, help me become more interested in Jesus."

RECEIVE Christ's Invitation by finding the gift that falls into the lap of those who long for it.

RESPOND by Inviting a friend the way Jesus would. Who will you Invite?

RENEW your mind by reading books by Chuck Colson and Philip Yancey.

Chapter 2

FOLLOWING THE LEADER

The next day Jesus decided to leave for Galilee. Finding Philip, he said to him, "Follow me."

Philip, like Andrew and Peter, was from the town of Bethsaida. Philip found Nathanael and told him, "We have found the one Moses wrote about in the Law, and about whom the prophets also wrote—Jesus of Nazareth, the son of Joseph."

"Nazareth! Can anything good come from there?" Nathanael asked.

"Come and see," said Philip.

When Jesus saw Nathanael approaching, he said of him, "Here is a true Israelite, in whom there is nothing false."

"How do you know me?" Nathanael asked.

Jesus answered, "I saw you while you were still under the fig tree before Philip called you."

Then Nathanael declared, "Rabbi, you are the Son of God; you are the King of Israel."

Jesus said, "You believe because I told you I saw you under the fig tree. You shall see greater things than that."[1]

—St. John

> What are we to make of Christ? There is no question of what we can make of Him, it is entirely a question of what He intends to make of us. You must accept or reject the story.[2]
>
> —C. S. Lewis

> In most societies there is always a group of people who are on the verge of converting to Christianity, and their openness to it involves both intellectual and attitudinal factors.[3]
>
> John Wimber

"A Woman's Place is in the Mall"
"Born to Shop"

Bumper stickers proclaim the philosophy of our times. At least through the eyes of some. Shopping serves as an escape for many: a coping skill requiring only a place to shop and either large amounts in bank accounts or loads of will power.

Despite the trend, I am not and have never been a happy shopper. I reluctantly accompany my wife on mall excursions when my excuses grow lame. Or maybe after reading a convicting book about husbands loving their wives and all that stuff. My demeanor, though, convinces her to invite a more willing participant for such trips. Unless I linger in bookstores or sports' shops, I grow weary in my attempt at well-doing.

I've really always been like that. In my childhood my Mother took me shopping, leaving me with less of a choice than I have now. On one of my dreaded childhood shopping adventures in a small Georgia town, I endured an experience that may not have increased my distaste for shopping but most certainly flavored my idea of evangelism.

Mama eyed racks in the clothing department. I fidgeted and squirmed until she allowed me to go next door to the toy store.

Before I made my way into the better place, a monster attacked me. Honest. Not a fire-breathing dragon. Not a one-eyed ogre. Just close.

The monster was a preacher. Complete with an oversized, bright red Bible, pink polyester leisure suit (with yellow tie), large white shoes, stacks of tracts, and a booming voice. He was big. From my vantage point he appeared both mean and mad. I was small. I was scared. He grabbed the sleeve of my Atlanta Braves T-shirt, handed me a gospel pamphlet and popped the question, "Boy, have you been saved or would you go to hell if you died today?"

That's what I remember. I'm sure upon my escape I felt overjoyed to return to the ladies' clothing department where my Mama could protect me from the fire-breathing, loud-shouting, angry-looking evangelist. I attended church regularly, knew about Jesus and hell, but I could not make a connection between Jesus and that preacher.

Don't get me wrong. I'm in favor of tracts and street preaching. I've witnessed that way many times. I know, though, that I wasn't drawn closer to Christ that day. Filled with fear? Yes. Following up with faith? No.

As we seek to influence others for Christ, why can't we follow the Leader? Wouldn't it work best to do things the way Jesus did? I would rather learn from Him than emulate the techniques of over-eager used-car salesmen. This second Invitation of Jesus paints a lovely picture of how evangelism worked for the Master Evangelist.

JESUS FINDS PHILIP

Our previous story ended with Jesus speaking to Peter, who had been brought to Christ by Andrew. Like the cycle of evaporation and precipitation, the life-style evangelism cycle continues in this narrative. Jesus reached out to Philip. Philip subsequently reached out to Nathanael.

Unlike the buttonholing preacher, Jesus expanded His ministry team with kindness. He gently, directly called Peter to follow Him. We notice no hesitancy in Philip. Jesus called. He responded. We must remember Jesus didn't always enjoy amiable audiences and neither will we.

We should also notice an important theological truth at work in this encounter. Ever heard of prevenient grace? That concept is often forgotten in the arena of modern evangelicalism. Prevenient grace is the grace preceding a conversion experience. It is God preparing and drawing a sinner closer to salvation. Grace at conversion is great. So is the continuing grace to follow that event. But we often ignore the grace preparing us for those steps.

How did Jesus describe prevenient grace? He said, "No man can come unto me unless the Father who sent me draws him."[4] Contemporary outreach efforts fail to stress this vital dynamic. Salvation is God's work. On those occasions when we are allowed to play small roles in His operation, we must keep our efforts in perspective. Human words and witness and work only go so far. God's Spirit draws humans supernaturally, a feat impossible in our own strength, style, technique.

A.W. Tozer captures the thought:

"Christian theology teaches the doctrine of prevenient grace, which briefly stated means this, that before a man can seek God, God must first have sought the man."[5]

Maybe the "I Found It" bumper stickers should be replaced with "I've Been Found." Philip would agree. Being found by Jesus thrust him into the reality of following the Leader. The True Leader.

As in our first Invitation, following Christ means more than organizing one's thoughts in a way that concludes: "Yes, He is who He says." It goes drastically farther than emotionally responding to a moving appeal. Following Christ is not a momentary restructuring of the habits and hopes of our lives. While it does not require complete understanding of all present realities and future ramifications, following Christ is saying YES with all that we are.

To follow Jesus means to:

- observe Him
- shadow Him
- pursue Him
- imitate Him
- reflect Him

By requesting Philip's and our presence on His mission, Christ offers humans an opportunity to experience life in a new way, on a New Way.

"Follow me." See those two words as an offer, not an order. Not a threat to "come or else," but an opportunity difficult to turn down. "Come along," Invited Jesus, "and be a part of a brand new existence."

PHILIP FINDS NATHANAEL

Remember Andrew racing to find Simon and tell him about Jesus? Philip's initial act in his new life of following the Inviter reminds us of that. It was "the first thing Andrew did."[6] Philip, likewise, spread the news. He found Nathanael. He restrained neither his words nor his enthusiasm in attempting to convince Nathanael that Jesus was more than a man. The one who had been found became a finder of others.

People devote time, energy, money and conversations to the causes they believe in, experiences they enjoy. An avid sports fan devours certain pages in the paper or sites on the web or channels on cable everyday. Box scores and pitching match-ups and trade rumors.

The social activist? Placards carried. Articles clipped. Talk shows watched and called. Websites visited and messages sent. Opinions voiced and debates argued.

A new grandmother? An ample supply of baby pictures. Humorous "guess what my grandbaby's doing now" stories always on hand. Debates about appearance, resemblance, rules, future plans.

We become obsessed often. The passions vary, touching every possible interest.

Whatever we become absorbed by is what we speak of and think about most often.

For Philip, conversation accentuated his new Leader. He was absorbed by his new way of life. It is, however, theoretically possible that his eagerness to enlist Nathanael grew out of the newness of his own experience. Jesus impressed him. Philip enjoyed the honeymoon emotions of a fresh, untarnished relationship. Such a motivation—while possible and probable—can't fully account for the strength of Philip's pronouncement.

Men of Philip's caliber tend not to shout "Messiah" simply when fascinated by another person. Philip's initial preoccupation with Christ and his future proximity to Christ stemmed from an awareness of being found. Philip's search for Truth came up empty until Truth found him. Through that simple, growing conviction came an earnest determination to think about Jesus and speak of Jesus.

He began his proclamation by joining His audience in their place. Philip found Nathanael where Nathanael was. Philip appealed to Scripture: "Moses wrote of Him. The prophets foretold His coming. Now He's here. It's Jesus of Nazareth, the Son of Joseph."

Nathanael, an Israelite, knew the prophecies of the promised Messiah. By beginning there, Philip left no doubt about his message. He didn't mumble about Jesus being a nice guy. He didn't delay words, depending on Nathanael's response. He stated his case. Clearly. Correctly. I'm sure he still didn't understand everything. But he confidently clarified his view: "Jesus is the Messiah."

Nathanael's response sprouted from a seed of prejudice planted within his mind. He had doubted as to whether even a well-meaning person could hail from Nazareth. Certainly not a Messiah. People are said to be prejudiced when they form their opinions prior to knowing the facts. Or when they hold to their belief in disregard of facts that contradict that belief. Every person we encounter owns some measure of prejudice. Most choose to be less open about it than Nathanael. Our assumptions can block receptivity to any message of good news.

In that setting Philip responded appropriately. He gave a glimpse of how to counter someone's deeply held judgments. He said, "Come and see."

There is a time and place for apologetics. Arguing, defending and proving Christianity are proper when kept in perspective. Throughout this book, we will notice ways to be sure and mention ministries who can help in that area. Nothing, though, compares to saying, "Let me take you to Jesus. You have to see Him for yourself."

In Christianity, objective faith—as in Philip's words regarding Scripture—combines with subjective experience—as in the admonition to "come and see"—to confirm reality. Without a knowledge of Truth, experience can hardly be trusted. Without an experience with the Truth, facts remain cold and distant. Philip led Nathanael toward both.

NATHANAEL FINDS JESUS

Nathanael approached Jesus. Jesus spoke first. His words permitted Nathanael to know that—at least from Christ's vantage point—the two were not strangers. By Jesus, the One he doubted, Nathanael was known. Christ spoke, disarming Nathanael with frankness. Upon learning Jesus' knowledge predated Philip's invitation, his jaw dropped open. His defenses fell. His prejudice crumbled, leaving him in awe. In one sentence he confessed three facets of the diamond of Truth. He labeled Jesus as:

1 Rabbi
2. Son of God
3. King of Israel

Addressing Jesus as "Rabbi" wasn't unusual. By calling Him "Son of God" and "King of Israel" Nathanael revealed a change of heart. His skepticism gave way to faith: a belief yet in its infancy, but real faith. Nathanael's partial understanding of the person of Christ did not diminish the intensity of his confession. He found Jesus. Not to be another of the many false Christs or fanatics produced by Nazareth, but to be the long awaited Rescuer of God's people.[7]

Jesus alluded to a great adventure awaiting both Philip and Nathanael when He said they would see "greater things than that."[8] At that point, though, a complete turn in the cycle of evangelism had been completed. Jesus found Philip who found Nathanael who found Jesus to be who Philip claimed. What a glorious pattern for us to observe and emulate.

Since statistics tell us that 86% of converts were invited to Christ by a friend or relative,[9] we would be foolish to not follow the model of Jesus, of Philip. Not only is the technique biblical. It works.

The book *Life-Style Evangelism* by Joe Aldrich defines and explains this evangelistic pattern. He leads Christians to act in world changing ways. Those who read the book will be stirred to reach out to people in biblically sound and practically effective ways. In the introduction, Aldrich whets the reader's appetite for life-style evangelism with an intriguing story. It is a fitting conclusion to this Invitation of Jesus:

> "There is a legend which recounts the return of Jesus to glory after His time on earth. Even in heaven He bore the marks of His earthly pilgrimage with its cruel cross and shameful death. The angel Gabriel approached Him and said, 'Master, you must have suffered terribly for me down there.'
>
> 'I did,' He said.
>
> 'And,' continued Gabriel, 'do they know all about how you loved them and what you did for them?'
>
> 'Oh, no,' said Jesus, 'not yet. Right now only a handful of people in Palestine know.
>
> Gabriel was perplexed. 'Then what have you done,' he asked, 'to let everyone know about your love for them?'
>
> Jesus said, 'I've asked Peter, James, John, and a few more friends to tell other people about Me. Those who are told will in turn tell still other people about Me, and My story will be spread to the farthest reaches of the globe. Ultimately, all of mankind will have heard about My life and what I have done.'
>
> Gabriel frowned and looked rather skeptical. He knew well what poor stuff men were made of. 'Yes,' he said, 'but what if Peter and James and John grow weary? What if the people who come after them forget? What if way down in the twentieth century, people just don't tell others about you? Haven't you made other plans?'
>
> And Jesus answered, 'I haven't made any other plans. I'm counting on them.'

Twenty centuries later…He still has no other plan. He's counting on you and me."[10]

REJOICE that this ministry helps share the Invitation: The mission of Teams Commissioned for Christ International (TCCI) is to equip and send short-term missions teams into the foreign field. TCCI is the producer of the exclusive GO Prepared short-term missions video training series, designed to equip individuals and teams of all types to engage in a meaningful and productive short-term missions experience. The series is comprehensive, practical, inspirational and creative, and features internationally recognized missions leaders. For more information or to preview the GO Prepared series contact TCCI at: www.tcci.org

RELEASE your worries by praying, "God, assist me in hearing Christ's welcome today in a new way."

RECEIVE Christ's Invitation by accepting the opportunity you can hardly turn down.

RESPOND by Inviting a friend the way Jesus would. Who will you Invite?

RENEW your mind by reading books by Frederick Buechner, Timothy Jones, Gordon MacDonald and Annie Dillard.

Chapter 3

GONE FISHIN'

As Jesus was walking beside the Sea of Galilee, he saw two brothers, Simon called Peter and his brother Andrew. They were casting a net into the lake, for they were fishermen. "Come, follow me," Jesus said, "and I will make you fishers of men." At once they left their nets and followed him.

Going on from there, he saw two other brothers, James son of Zebedee and his brother John. They were in a boat with their father Zebedee, preparing their nets. Jesus called them, and immediately they left the boat and their father and followed him.

Jesus went throughout Galilee, teaching in their synagogues, preaching the good news of the kingdom, and healing every disease and sickness among the people. News about him spread all over Syria, and people brought to him all who were ill with various diseases, those suffering severe pain, the demon-possessed, those having seizures, and the paralyzed, and he healed them.[1]

—Matthew the Tax Collector

But the Lord God called to the man, "Where are you?"[2]

—God to Adam in the Garden

> In solitude we take some distance from the many opinions and ideas of our fellow human beings and become vulnerable to God. There we can listen carefully to him and distinguish between our desires and our task, between our urges and our vocation, between the cravings of our heart and the call of God.[3]
> —Henri J. M. Nouwen

The evangelist stands poised at the podium edge, pleading for sinners to come forward. The atmosphere charged with emotion, he passionately appeals to the crowd packing the stadium. Christians pray. Friends agree to wait. Music adjusts the mood as the choir sings "Just As I Am." Soon people cover the field. Seekers hope to find answers and counselors assist those pursuing help.

Are you familiar with that scene? Countless converts have prayed the "sinner's prayer" at such gatherings. Analysts question long-term effectiveness of mass evangelism, and we all know those who once walked down but later walked away from their New Friend. We can't deny, though, the good achieved and the lives enriched.

That method of offering an Invitation still works. So do many others. What Christendom lacks in power we attempt to offset with an endless array of techniques "guaranteed" to reach large numbers of new believers. Those we call "lost" are the ones we pray shall be found. We try many ways to notify them of "The Way":

- Music groups of every style combine gospel words with a myriad of rhythms to reach every potential audience.
- Movie stars, athletes and politicians travel the circuit telling their "born again" stories.
- Zealous believers carry crosses, wear shirts bearing catchy slogans, don multi-colored wigs and leave tracts in any place possible, hoping to bring people to Jesus.

- Strong, handsome muscle men break boards and blocks of ice while testifying of God's power to save.
- Church groups gather across the land at appointed times and hear speakers conclude sermons by instructing sinners to come forward, raise a hand, stand up, nod a head, sign a card or remain silent to signify acceptance of the message presented.
- Internet connections, mission trips, seeker friendly churches, café churches, house churches, television shows, radio programs, book deals, magazine articles, musical styles, drama, evangelism classes, conventions, prayer walks, posters, parables, videos: the list goes on.

None work as perfectly as we wish. Since participants include people like us, results fall far short of our dreams. But we still dream. We still hope. We still act with energy and sincerity. Some leaders stumble and some ministries make mistakes. The end does not justify faulty means, but most methods are better than no ministry at all.

But how can we improve? We spend time, energy, resources. We say what we think God wants us to say. We pray for individuals, people groups and nations. Still, we want more to not miss the glory of His grace. So, what lessons lead us toward better ways of Inviting people to enter the Kingdom for the long term?

Maybe we should pause. Maybe even exit the treadmill long enough to compare our approaches with the Invitations of Jesus. Maybe new answers follow this question: How did Jesus Invite them?

Let's continue the journey back in time to observe Christ's Invitations, traveling 2000 years in reverse to the shores of the Sea of Galilee. No choirs or cameras. No media blitz or highlight hits. Only Jesus and a few fishermen. The sight? The smell? A little different from modern stage productions. The stink set the scene for reality. It was another day in the life of normal people. And another day in the Life of Jesus.

The fishermen, Simon and Andrew, "were not decrepit men with gray beards and bent backs so often depicted in paintings....Rather, these were rough, tough young men at the powerful peak of early manhood, either in their late teens or early twenties."4

As we learned in A Simple Invitation, Andrew came to Christ through the witness of John the baptizer. He then introduced Simon to Jesus. Then they returned to their work as "partners with James and John in Zebedee's fishing business."5 Jesus saw them fishing. He voiced His Invitation: "Come, follow me and I will make you fishers of men."

INVITATION

Once again Jesus swung open the door to Life by speaking the word "come." To the young fishermen, Jesus said, "Come." Inviting them to approach Him, to be with Him. Think about it. Did He ask them, "Will you come?" Did He tone it as an exclamation: "Come!"?

However the word sounded, Jesus had seen them before. Remember? At the first meeting Andrew asked Jesus where He was staying. Jesus answered, "Come and see." What a personal Invitation! Not "What is it to you?" or "Call my office" or "I can see you next Thursday at 10:00." Just, "Come on over and see for yourself."

Jesus showed personal attention. He spoke specifically rather than voicing a general welcome cloaked in religious jargon. Andrew was a person to Christ, not a pawn in the game of amassing a substantial following. A person.

At that encounter Andrew stayed with Jesus for the remainder of that day. He came away so impressed that he told Simon he had found the Messiah. In this chapter's narrative, Jesus didn't ask them why they returned to fishing. He didn't rebuke or question. He played no game of conversational tag.

He merely Invited them. "Come," He said. "Be with me. See where I live, see how I live, see why I live. Come witness My behavior." A simple, concise, stirring Invitation.

EXHORTATION

Jesus then expanded the Invitation by qualifying the welcome. He encouraged them to not only come but to follow Him. They weren't to come to Him without a purpose or plan of involvement once they arrived at the destination. A journey toward Christ develops into a life of following Him. Noticing isn't enough. Observing isn't enough. As mentioned earlier, "to follow" means to come after, to become an adherent, to pattern one's steps after. "Come hear me preach, then go back as you came" wasn't the strategy. By saying, "Come, follow me," Jesus implied, "Come and be a part of what I'm doing in the earth; join your life with Mine."

Amazingly they did it. They left their nets at once and followed Him. The word translated "left" was used elsewhere to speak of dismissing a wife for the purpose of divorce. It was also used to mean forgiving sins completely. So they divorced their nets and followed Jesus. In doing so, those two young brothers—one of whom was married—left what was possibly the only occupation they had ever known or considered. They turned their backs. On their income. On their security. Why? To follow a Man who traveled from town to town telling folksy stories.

Doesn't sound very intelligent, does it?

Likewise, James and John climbed out of their boats and onto the path of Jesus. "Immediately" they left their nets and their father. Inherent in this biblical concept of following was the reality of leaving behind.

In today's society following Christ is presented as a means of enhancing one's present lifestyle rather than a radical call to exit that lifestyle. Many hear the "come" but turn deaf ears to the "follow me." What good is the coming without the following? Would a bride leave a wedding ceremony where she pledged her total commitment to a groom, then return home, stay with Mom and Dad, and continue living the way she had lived previously? The welcome includes both the Invitation to come and the exhortation to follow. Neglecting either aspect leaves a person outside the fullness of what Christ longs to, and loves to, bring.

TRANSFORMATION

Subsequent to the Invitation and exhortation we notice a promise of transformation. Christ's equation of reception equals this third component, which served as the by-product of a proper response to the two initial factors:

Come + Follow Me = I Will Make You Fishers of Men

Jesus vowed to give New Life to those who gave their existing lives to Him. Why come and follow? Is there a valid reason here? To the followers, Christ pledges to rearrange their lives. He guaranteed to transform fishermen into men fishers.

Many teachers then and many teachers now voice similar, but drastically different, arrangements for their followers. I've heard it. I've read it. I also have written it and said it myself. In my desire to declare truth, in my yearning to rescue lives, I must admit it: I haven't always done it Christ's way.

We might Invite and exhort and encourage transformation. Good plan. But the procedures to promote how such change can be realized are emphatically distinct from the means of change in Christ's declaration. We might teach students to follow their precepts, changing themselves through inner resolve and determination until they could conform to the desired code.

Not so with Jesus. While He expected obedience, He promised to bring about the change Himself. And He still does. In the lives of those aligning with Him, Jesus assumes responsibility of the makeover, of the re-creating, of the amending. "I will make you what I want you to be," says that Messiah.

The New Testament word translated "make" means to produce something or to endow a person with a certain quality. Emphasis rests on the subject, not the means.[6] In the story we have no organ music. No moving anecdote. No holy pause. Just an Invitation, an exhortation, and a promise of transformation. Jesus assured them He would make them different. His statement wasn't a command to change. It was a commitment to work His change within them. He pledged to transform His followers into effective people reachers and world changers.

Gone Fishin'

In the transformation process—a much more gradual one than we would prefer—three truths can serve to encourage us. Instead of expecting and focusing on sudden alteration, maybe we should meditate on the way He:

- Sees us
- Saves us
- Sends us

He sees us as people, not as numbers. He knows each address, phone number, financial portfolio. The oil in our engines and the gas in our tanks. He knows our every thought. He even knows the hair on my head, how much has fallen out, how long it was during my preacher-can-still-find-ways-to-rebel days, how much my stylist cuts, and the rays of the sun's reflection from my bald, bold head. What a view He has!

We are individuals in His eyes. We have potential. He believes in what He can do with us.

In His first meeting with Simon, Jesus revealed how He saw the young fisherman by announcing, "I'm gonna call you Rock." Would the Pharisees' Board of Strategic Planning have seen Simon as possessing such promise? Would we? Seaweed maybe. But Rock? Never. Jesus saw him as "Rock."

We are all influenced by others' perceptions of us. When my oldest son Taylor was young, his Mom hugged him early one morning. "You're so cute," Debbie said.

Taylor responded, "Why do you always call me cute? I don't want to be cute."

Shocked by his reply, Debbie asked, "Well, what do you want to be?"

He said, "I want to be like Daddy. Just plain."

In my son's eyes I was "just plain." Certainly not cute. Fortunately Christ sees us as much more than plain. It is because of His perception of us that a hope of transformation—true and lasting—can birth.

He not only sees us, He saves us. I'm glad God loves me just as I am. I'm significantly more awed by the fact that He chooses to do something about the way I am. Accepting me as I am now is great as a starting point. But I need more. I need to be rescued from the way I am. Why? Though He accepts me, I remain unacceptable in an eternal sense. He commits Himself to rescue and restore those willing to come ashore.

Peter and Andrew returned again to fishing at some point after that encounter. Luke records, in chapter five of his account, that Jesus approached them and directed them to a fishing jackpot. There the Savior altered His phrasing to reemphasize His purpose for their lives: "Don't be afraid. From now on you will catch men."[7]

Jesus can save us from our sins, from ourselves, from living lives of going through the motions, from being too intimidated to launch out into the depths of Life. And He doesn't give up on us easily.

Sees us. Saves us. Then, He sends us out into the lake of humanity as a new breed of fishermen. The group floats out, called to echo the Invitation Jesus graciously gave. The ticket needed to enter the journey is this: all those who come and follow qualify for Jesus to direct them into the destiny He has designed.

Come to Jesus. Follow Him. Be made new. Not bad, is it?

Peter, Andrew, James and John probably hung a "Gone Fishin'" sign over their boat. What a unique place for such an announcement. It didn't signify that they had chosen a different boat for the day's excursion. Nor that they had gone on vacation. The "Gone Fishin'" sign said they had met Someone who had promised to change their lives forever and change the forever of their lives.

Doesn't His Invitation still ring out? Isn't it just as real and personal to us today as it was when Jesus welcomed His disciples by the water?

They left all they knew. They left all they were. They said, "Yes. We're in."

I want to listen and hear. I want to respond again.

Maybe I should hang a "Gone Fishin'" sign on the vestiges of my past. What about you? Want to set sail?

As those caught we can become those who catch. Then we can go after a person. Not masses. Just individuals. This one. Then that one.

When they see us and hear us and notice our enjoyment of the journey, maybe the masses will slowly come in.

REJOICE that this ministry helps share the Invitation: Campus Crusade for Christ applies these principles in a variety of ways. Through their ministries in 2001, more than 677.3 million people heard Jesus Invite them, and 17.6 million accepted those Invitations. Since its beginning in 1951 under the vision of Bill Bright, more than 6.7 billion have heard the Invitation worldwide. And, since 1979, 4.5 billion Beggars have been Invited to Jesus through the JESUS film—a film that has been seen in every country of the world and translated into 712 languages.

www.ccci.org

RELEASE your worries by praying, "God, lure me away from my habit of fishing and into a lifetime of fishing with Jesus."

RECEIVE Christ's Invitation by getting rid of any nets holding you back.

RESPOND by Inviting a friend the way Jesus would. Who will you Invite?

RENEW your mind by reading books written by Bill Bright, Josh McDowell and James Kennedy's "Evangelism Explosion."

Chapter 4

EXCUSES, EXCUSES

When Jesus saw the crowd around him, he gave orders to cross to the other side of the lake. Then a teacher of the law came to him and said, "Teacher, I will follow you wherever you go."

Jesus replied, "Foxes have holes and birds of the air have nests, but the Son of Man has no place to lay his head."

Another disciple said to him, "Lord, first let me go and bury my father."

But Jesus told him, "Follow me, and let the dead bury their own dead."[1]
—Matthew the Tax Collector

Jesus is just alright with me.[2]
—The Doobie Brothers

A spoonful of sugar helps the medicine go down.[3]
—Mary Poppins

My children love to take certain types of medicine. The reason? The medicine they enjoy tastes like fruit punch. Vitamins aren't a problem; they taste like candy. No coercion needed to force them in brushing teeth when toothpaste is bubble gum flavored.

Oh, the signs of the times. Chores I despised as a kid have been made pleasurable by marketing experts. They know certain flavors translate into sure sales. Parents don't mind. It beats bitter confrontations.

Making tasks more desirable, however, may have invented a dangerous tendency. Minds now doubt the value of experiences equaling both necessary and unpleasant. We become spoiled by immediate gratification of enjoyable experiences. Hard work? A stranger unless rewards arrive rapidly and lavishly. Tackling unpleasant tasks first? An archaic philosophy. Pleasure equals both the end and the means these days. If something feels good we conclude it must be beneficial.

If we aren't careful that principle could spill into our evangelistic thrusts. We could begin to preach a Jesus of our own making instead of the Real King. We could sugarcoat His hard sayings in an attempt to make them more palatable to the masses. We could stress easy believism in order to fill our auditoriums, expand our mailing lists and enlarge our funds. Scary, isn't it?

F. F. Bruce should serve as a caveat to modern American Christians:

> "It is all too easy to believe in a Jesus who is largely a construction of our own imagination—an inoffensive person whom no one would really trouble to crucify. But the Jesus whom we meet in the Gospels, far from being an inoffensive person, gave offense right and left. Even his loyal followers found him, at times, thoroughly disconcerting. He upset all established notions of religious propriety. He spoke of God in terms of intimacy which sounded like blasphemy. He seemed to enjoy the most questionable company. He set out with open eyes on a road which, in the view of 'sensible people,' was bound to lead to disaster."[4]

Yet, our Jesus fits our world. He is in step with the times. We have made Him a yuppie executive more concerned with bottom lines than broken lives. I think about me. Would I dare to discourage someone from following Christ? Do I really encourage listeners to count the cost?

The Master Inviter, when faced with two potential converts in this narrative, served the medicine plain. No sugar added. He didn't seem to operate as "sweet little Jesus." He acted like a leader possessing insight behind the customary iron curtains of people. He revealed reality. He offered it to those who dared to investigate. Notice three reality-centered questions He asked His seekers.

WHAT ARE THE PROPS OF YOUR LIFE?

A scribe came to Jesus. This expert in the law offered to follow Him anywhere. Most leaders would love to add an educated, capable teacher to their ministry team. Jesus never shifted into the recruiter mode. Status, reputation and talent didn't impress Him. He cut through words. He attacked motives.

Using the title Son of Man—the name underscoring His humiliation—Jesus informed the scribe that He had no permanent mailing address, that His mission afforded not even the promise of consistent shelter.

Does His reply seem cruel to such an earnest searcher?

> "It is less cruel to disillusion such a man than to let him rush in and go down in disappointment. Jesus neither accepts or declines his offer. His reply strikes at the heart of the matter; the man must see what his offer involves, not in idealism, but in sober, sane realism."[5]

By His statement Jesus proved He wasn't a polished politician unrealistically promising to make His followers the healthiest, wealthiest and wisest people of the world. His agenda wasn't compatible with the greed, laziness and narcissism society exhibited.

Jesus said, "Here are the facts. I want you to know what you're getting into. Think it over."

Today Christ's method and message remain the same. I prefer comfort instead of a cross. The Way of Christ leads down many lonely roads until it consummates under a darkened sky at a hill called The Skull. Isn't it funny how such thought rarely makes it to the religious section of local papers, where church ads try to prove how "our church is better than your church"?

Jesus asked potential followers, "What are your props? Do you want Me or what you sense I can add to your already oversized collection of toys? What are your security blankets?"

How appropriate these questions become to my country, my life, my selfishness. My world remains enamored with having more and sacrificing less. What do we depend upon for happiness and fulfillment? One in four Americans suffer from codependency, an addiction to people, things or behaviors. Our family members, our friends and ourselves might find our names on such a list.

Jesus attacked the support system of cumbersome lives. He didn't add to it. He wanted it changed. The Good News is bad news for hedonism: the Kingdom offer promises no immediate gratification of selfish desires. What does it do then? It holds high the example:

- A God becoming baby
- A Divine Being living on earth as a wandering, meek, homeless servant
- A Creator and Owner of the world becoming a rejected, killed victim

WHAT IS THE PRIORITY OF YOUR LIFE?

First we have a scribe who "was overready and had to be cautioned." Now we see a disciple (how long an adherent we don't know) who "wants to delay and join Jesus later."[6] Commentators disagree as to whether the man's father was really dead. If so, the delay would have been short. If he was still alive, the disciple meant he needed to wait until his father passed away and all family obligations satisfied before he committed himself to traveling with Jesus.

In either case Jesus did not oppose family responsibility or involvement. As with many of His statements, we have no indication He said this to anyone else. The intent, though, seems to echo in all His teaching: "Rank the Kingdom first." Christ had no desire to make followers cruel and uncaring to family and friends, but He wanted to highlight the ultimate importance of His supreme mission. Those interested in joining that mission needed to realize that the "decision, when it comes, demands obedience which is...without condition."[7]

In Luke's account, a third and similar narrative joined these two. This time, a man wanted to say good-bye to his family prior to joining the Revolution. Jesus responded, delivering His famous and usually taken out of context quote: "No one who puts his hand to the plow and looks back is fit for service in the Kingdom of God."[8]

That further stresses the point of the priority of Jesus' plan. The wording refers to a beginner who is setting his hand to the plow for the first time and "indicates, not an occasional glance backward, but a constant looking at the rear."[9]

Jesus held no animosity toward family relationships or funeral obligations. We can relate to the self-serving, guilt-alleviating sentimentality that surfaces after a death. People who hardly knew the deceased decide to shower a family with meals, flowers, cards and tears. Jesus said, "Concern yourself with the living. Time is short. We have miles to travel, miracles to give, hearts to heal. Make following me the priority. Or don't follow me at all."

WHAT IS THE PURPOSE OF YOUR LIFE?

The first two questions point together to this third, overriding question. Jesus pierced pious phrasing. He shattered superficial slogans. He questioned props and priorities because those issues reveal the real us. That real purpose. That deep, inner motivation silently steering us. Not our stated or well-rehearsed purpose. Jesus hears our words. He also sees carefully hidden agendas. He sees where our security dwells, how we seek to see it swell.

I need frequent reviews of my motives, my longings, my trends. Habits not only haunt us. They announce what tries to hide inside us. They expose the people or tasks or chores I pursue while putting my following Jesus agenda on pause. To test myself and to help friends test themselves, lists like this can help:

- Record every financial expense for a month to reveal how you spend money
- Track a schedule of fifteen-minute segments to jot how you spend time
- List the nouns of people and places and events which mean more to you than Jesus does
- List the verbs of actions you could do to make needed changes
- Ask a few friends to give you their opinions of what means the most to you

Stirring those exercises into the pot of introspection can bring surprises. It shows us much. Maybe too much. Especially if we compare results to this popular, but often ignored, statement of Jesus: "But seek first his kingdom and his righteousness, and all these things will be given to you as well."[10]

Props? Seek first His kingdom and His righteousness, and *all these things will be given to you as well.* Contrary to the popular teaching of the "positive faith" proponents, Christianity is not a meal ticket to the best the world has to offer. It does make us eligible to have our needs met,[11] but satisfying fleshly desire is the last thing God wants to do. All we truly need, though, will be supplied. Our wants might get in the way while God plans to send a supply of real needs our way.

Priority? Seek *first* His kingdom and His righteousness. We need to make these objects of seeking, pursuing, longing for, craving, the priorities of life. Not items high up on our Top Ten Priority List. The priorities. What if we refused to automatically paste other activities under that Number One Goal? What if we only included life's aspects as a part of that, not a separate item? Maybe if we did, those which couldn't fit would be deleted, discarded, destroyed.

Purpose? *Seek* first *His kingdom and His righteousness.* Seek? It means to strive for, aim at, wish for, try to obtain. Making that the purpose of life means letting go of the props, changing the priority and joining forces with the King who has plans for this place, the King who has a place for us in His plans.

Keith Green pledged his head, his wife, his son to heaven for the gospel.[12] If I made his song personal, what should I write?

Mark Twain confessed that the "things in the Bible that bothered him the most were not the things he did not understand but those that he did understand."[13] I hope we understand enough of this story to be bothered by it. The only times it hasn't bothered me are the times I've read through it so quickly that I didn't let it climb into my heart. I made it keep a distance.

What if we receive the challenge to look deep within? To answer tough questions? To give honest answers? To readjust our lives? I pray we will follow Jesus, taking care to know what we are getting into while choosing to place our hand on the plow anyway. Maybe we will never look back. Maybe we will never let go. And maybe, when observers notice our dedication, they'll also climb on board and leave behind whatever doesn't belong.

REJOICE that this ministry helps share the Invitation: Is language of the Bible an excuse? Wycliffe Bible Translations is doing something about it. Something great! More than 380 million people worldwide still need God's Word in their language. At the current rate of translation, they would have to wait for another 100 to 150 years. That's too long! Wycliffe's mission is to assist the church in making disciples of all nations through Bible translation. Their vision is to see translation in progress among every language group that needs it by 2025. Vision 2025 is a vision for all of God's church. It is not a program or campaign. It is a call to commitment. You are Invited to join them. www.wycliffe.org

RELEASE your worries by praying, "God, change my goals from immediate gratification to eternal joy."

RECEIVE Christ's Invitation by listing your past excuses and throwing that list away.

RESPOND by Inviting a friend the way Jesus would. Who will you Invite?

RENEW your mind by reading books by Joseph Aldrich, Robert Coleman and Rick Warren.

Chapter 5

A Familiar Face in a Frightening Place

One day Jesus said to his disciples, "Let's go over to the other side of the lake." So they got into a boat and set out. As they sailed, he fell asleep. A squall came down on the lake, so that the boat was being swamped, and they were in great danger.

The disciples went and woke him, saying, "Master, Master, we're going to drown!"

He got up and rebuked the wind and the raging waters; the storm subsided, and all was calm.

"Where is your faith?" he asked his disciples.

In fear and amazement they asked one another, "Who is this? He commands even the winds and the water, and they obey him."[1]

—Luke the Physician

No one will be able to stand up against you all the days of your life. As I was with Moses, so I will be with you; I will never leave you nor forsake you.

"Be strong and courageous, because you will lead these people to inherit the land I swore to their forefathers to give them. Be strong and very courageous. Be careful to obey all the law my servant Moses gave you; do not turn from it to the right or to the left, that you may be successful wherever you go.[2]

—Jehovah to Joshua after Moses' death

"All this I have spoken while still with you. But the Counselor, the Holy Spirit, whom the Father will send in my name, will teach you all things and will remind you of everything I have said to you. Peace I leave with you; my peace I give you. I do not give to you as the world gives. Do not let your hearts be troubled and do not be afraid.[3]

—Jesus the Christ, prior to His arrest

O ur ride now takes a turn. We move from confusing and misunderstood words of Jesus. We venture into a well-loved, exciting story.

Jesus calming the storm ranks behind few stories as a Sunday School, Children's Church, Sermon classic. Action-packed drama. Miraculous deliverance. Good triumphs over evil. Since in real life storms often crash the shores of our lives, knowing how Christ conquered the elements gives us hope.

Fear frequently visits. When we were young we feared monsters that were the stuffed animals we cherished only a few hours before bedrooms became dark. Heights, dogs, noises and dentists translate into rapid pulses and upset stomachs. Now older, the objects or causes of our fears have changed. Most people still live with fears housed in hidden closets of life.

All fear isn't bad. Some is healthy, necessary. We should fear an oncoming train enough to stay off the track. Or a handgun enough to never leave it loaded. We should fear God. These fears reveal a respect of the power or position of that which is feared. This respect, this fear, is legitimate. It must be kept in balance while not denied or avoided.

Unnecessary fears result more from problems within the one afraid than from potential harm inherent in the object. The event feared may be worthy of fear, though not in proportion to the fear possessed. Why is it with us? Fear of failure or desertion? Fear of tomorrow or tonight? Rejection? Loss of control? Mental and spiritual progress suffers from the crippling illness of unnecessary fear. God wants us released from fear unwelcome in His house of our lives.[4]

This story presents a case for victory. Triumph may be a stranger to us. If so, let's enter this scene anyway. Let's join in. Hearing the wind. Feeling the water. Swaying with the boat. Sensing the fear. Joining in a celebration as Christ brings a victory.

Sound fitting these days? Impossible?

Whether we feel handicapped by fear, darkened by evil forces appearing to be working overtime, or struggling through a situation where elements deserve a fearful respect, this story can help us adjust. It presents the proof of Christ's power. It calls us toward a courageous cure. And, if He is the same today as when the storm rocked His boat,[5] I think we need this ride.

PRESENCE

The story begins with words of Christ. His statement qualifies this narrative for a place among our Invitations: "Let's go over to the other side of the lake." I can sense warmth in the words of the Inviter. How do you think the disciples felt? By then they had understood a little bit of Jesus' Journey. They had seen His miracles. They had heard Him claim to be God. They responded when He invited them to join His team. And, as amazing as it might be for many to fathom, Jesus enjoyed being with them and Inviting them to go boating.

Invitations make us feel wanted, particularly when they come from one we admire. Knowing our presence is requested gives us cause for thinking that maybe we aren't as terrible or as unloved as our self-talk says. I'm sure the Pharisees questioned Jesus' choice of ministry leaders and, as such comments tend to do, doubts found their way to the ears of the blue-collar crusaders. Despite such sentiments, the Man who welcomed them wanted them. And they started their journey across the water.

What could have been a wonderful time of fellowship began turning sour from the start. The trip's Organizer fell asleep as they embarked. Exhausted from the endless stream of needy people, He hardly waited for all to board before finding a pillow and sailing into sleep.[6] Then a storm arose. Such weather hazards were common. The disciples probably didn't expect their parade to be rained on.

Frederick Buechner's words make the scene come to life:

> "He didn't doze off the bow where the spray would get him and the whitecaps slapped harder. He climbed back into the stern instead. There was a pillow under his head. Maybe somebody put it there for him. Maybe they didn't think to put it there till after he'd gone to sleep, and then somebody lifted his head a little off the hard deck and slipped it under.
>
> He must have gone out like a light because Mark says the storm didn't wake him, not even when the waves got so high they started washing in over the sides. They let him sleep on until finally they were so scared they couldn't stand it any longer and woke him up."[7]

The picture of Christ asleep on a pillow reveals His human side. He can relate to being worn out. Tired. In need of a break.

In the beautiful scene, there does appear to be something wrong with that picture. The sight would be more fitting if the boat had drifted peacefully through calm, clear waters. Jesus sleeping at a time like this seems rude. Lives were at stake and Jesus was on a momentary vacation. How could He sleep?

Let's focus on an important truth. Despite the fact that Jesus slept, He was still there with them. The first way Christ wants to

A Familiar Face in a Frightening Place

touch us in our place of fear is with His presence. We may immediately want His hand of deliverance. What we need most and what He never fails to bring is this: Himself. His hands at work are wonderful. But we need His face nearby more than His efforts, His achievements, His accomplishments.

The disciples felt in trouble. The text states they were in great danger. They weren't alone, though. Christ, while zonked, rode with them through the tempest. Does that mean He can be nearby during our storms, too? When bills mount and money drops, is He calm and close? When appliances all break down at once, is He on our couch enjoying a little R & R? When children rebel and resist and revolt, is He at peace amid those angry waves? When doctors bring bad news, is He snoring in the waiting room? If so, here is what I like. He is with us. We aren't alone.

God does work miracles. In anticipating the visible effects of His supernatural power, we often overlook the miracles of His consistent presence. Let's learn from some gossip about Him. He is our Great High Priest.[8] He promises to never desert His children.[9] He may be quiet, His presence unseen. Our prayers may seem directed to a Father who habitually sleeps. But we must walk by faith, not sight.[10] He is with us.

Can we ask for anything more wonderful? By gracing us with His presence Jesus gives the greatest gift of all. Even when other people offer us companionship instead of cliché-ridden comments, our lives find enrichment.

I remember one such person who helped me that way when my mother died. After a lengthy battle with cancer, she left me. I felt shattered. I appreciated the many words, cards, flowers and other expressions of condolence. During my grieving, a special friend taught me about the ministry of presence. We would climb in his car and ride in silence pierced only by sobs and questions.

I knew the theology of death and of life beyond. I didn't need answers. I didn't need advice. I needed a friend.

Too often we try to solve the problems of others with our clever words; like Job's helpers our wordiness frequently hinders more than helps. Trust me. I know. Sometimes the communicator in me preaches the counselor in me away and misses a time to care.

The ministry of presence touches hearts. My friend touched mine by caring.

In our story, Jesus ministered to the disciples by being with them. Through history His assistance has often stopped there. Martyrs die at the stake without deliverance, but not without Jesus nearby. We struggle with it, don't we? Planes crash. Haters rape innocent people. Foes invade nations. Bad things happen to all people. What should we do?

Remember from this story. Jesus isn't a fair-weather friend. He enters the storms of today just as He entered fire with Hebrew children.[11] The fire might feel hotter and the storm might sound louder. But He is with us.

PERSPECTIVE

His presence adds an interesting aspect to our perception of a dilemma. When we realize that we aren't alone, we can choose to begin viewing situations the way He does. We normally look at frightening and frustrating detours of life through lenses tinted by doubt and hopelessness. Unlimited by time, space and elements, Christ sees situations differently. The disciples failed to realize what Jesus knew: that being with Him in the place He wanted them was the safest place on earth. Jesus knew it. The teasing of the storm could not cloud His perspective.

I enjoy flying. A friend owns a plane and has flown me several times. Once we circled Orlando. Glancing down at Disney World, the "matter of perspective" hit me. I could see packed parking lots, long lines and impressive attractions. I viewed the sights much differently than the tourists and the characters could. I was able to see beyond the walls that blocked their vision. Flying above gave me a different vantage point. I traced where they had been, where they were then, what else was nearby, and where they were heading.

Obtaining God's perspective releases us from this assumption: for all to be well things must turn out the way we feel will be best. Because of walls we can't see over and because of corners we have yet to turn, we need the vantage point of God to anchor us in the storms of life.

Remember Joseph? He hardly felt the hand of God in the abuse of his brothers. Still, from the Higher Vantage Point, the plan for Joseph's life began to unfold.[12]

How can we exit myopia and look through lenses of eternity? How can we live fully in the present while noticing the everlasting? I wish I could offer a quick formula for success. Even our desire indicates our need for new glasses. No microwave version exists. Sudden changes usually swing us emotionally while failing to change our lives. Only true discipleship lived through prayer, meditation, worship, fellowship, Bible study and ministry, moves us toward obtaining proper perspective. Talking to and listening to God in silence? That helps. Reading Scripture and reaching out in service? Those help. When we view our storms from a lookout tower built upon:

- hours of studying the struggles of Apostle Paul,
- days of helping an elderly lady pay bills and purchase groceries,
- nights of staring at starry skies and acknowledging God's handiwork,
- and mornings of humbly submitting to private prayer...

our lives change

We become transformed. Patterns of thinking shift.[13] Like a traffic reporter in a helicopter, the traffic jams of life can be analyzed from above. Not beside or beneath. Jesus rebuked the disciples for their lack of faith. He protested their inclination to not let His presence affect their perspective. A change in perspective might have made the storm seem less threatening and made the boat feel more safe. After all, wasn't Christ still there with them?

POWER

Appreciate His presence. Achieve His perspective. Working on those principles will answer our prayers for assistance by changing us. Even if the situations stay stormy. We calm down. We look at it better.

Admit it, though. Often we need more.

And often, as in this story, Jesus stands to His feet and dramatically tampers with evidence. In their storm He shouted at the forces of nature. He commanded them to relinquish their destructive behavior. He loudly informed the violent disturbance that the time for a pause had come.

Would the wind dare to ignore a command from its very Breath? Would the sea rage on in defiance of an order from the One who scooped the water into the ancient basin?

Never. Nature is no match for words from His Mouth.

I love the wording of the text: "the storm subsided, and all was calm." How we long for such an outcome to our agony. Today, many of us feel sick from the waves. Today, when the toil and tension of hardships enslave us, Jesus can prevail.

Why doesn't He display His tremendous ability as frequently as we would prefer? I have an important answer for you. I don't know why. But I believe this: He is God. He does His will in His way at His time. The Problem Solver solves problems differently than how I instruct, plead, beg Him to.

What should I do about it? Keep instructing. Keep pleading. Keep begging. And keep trusting the real Know it All.

Reading Job might help. Job saw God's power to turn bad into good, dark into light. The manifestation didn't come through until lessons were learned. I need to remember that. Job needed to learn. We need to learn. God can teach us:

> "Can you make the mountains rise?
> Can you paint the morning skies?
> Were you here when the world began?
> Can you make the eagles soar?
> Can you make the ocean roar?
> Are you able to make humble man? I am."[14]

A Familiar Face in a Frightening Place

A storm can reveal God to us in ways trite sermons and trendy songs can't. Clutching the sides of a tossing boat until knuckles turn white and until stomachs turn inside out can preach premier theology. Ears and eyes open when trapped by desperation. Lessons are learned.

God turns the course of dilemma however He chooses. He is able. He is willing. Despite what a few dispensationalists say, miracles haven't ceased. Most doubters hope beliefs prove wrong when facing storms only miracles can quiet.

What can we do then? Maybe we can believe. Maybe we can refuse to deny the Weather Man's plan or the Wind Maker's power. While refusing to harness it and use it for ourselves, maybe His amazement is only one breeze away. I think He will do all that really needs to be done. And, even if He lets the boat ride a while before halting the tempest, I think it will be for our ultimate good.

I remember a radio advertisement inviting listeners to attend services at a local church. The tone sounded militant. The voice spoke a phrase that made me cringe: "Our church is not for the fainthearted." I think I know what they intended to say and I am in no way doubting their sincerity. But if the assembly of Christ's followers excludes the fainthearted, where can the fainthearted find comfort?

Storms are real. They frighten us. Hearts grow weak. Doubts come. Christ rebuked the fainthearted disciples, but He never turned them away. He stayed close. He provided presence, perspective, power.

For us He can do the same. Whatever storms or fears shake us and wake us, let's see His face in our frightening place.

He welcomes the fainthearted. He welcomes us. He longs to welcome our fearful friends. His presence is alive; His perspective accurate; His power awesome. No storm and no life should remain unaltered.

REJOICE that this ministry helps share the Invitation: Teen Challenge is the oldest, largest and most successful program of its kind in the world. Established in 1958 by David Wilkerson, Teen

Challenge has grown to more than 150 centers in the United States and 250 centers worldwide. Teen Challenge started as told in the book *The Cross and the Switchblade,* and offers a number of services to the community, many times free of charge. For over 40 years, Teen Challenge has been going into schools around the world working with teens to educate them about the dangers of drugs. Teen Challenge reaches out to people in juvenile halls, jails and prisons. The "jail teams" help show inmates there is hope for them to turn their lives around. And more importantly, they educate them in how to change their lives! www.teenchallenge.com

RELEASE your worries by praying, "God, remind me You are with me in today's storm."

RECEIVE Christ's Invitation by changing your perspective and receiving His power.

RESPOND by Inviting a friend the way Jesus would. Who will you Invite?

RENEW your mind by reading books by David Wilkerson, T.D. Jakes, Ted Haggard, Patrick Morley and Jim Cymbala.

Chapter 6

A Friend to the Friendless

As Jesus went on from there, he saw a man named Matthew sitting at the tax collector's booth. "Follow me," he told him, and Matthew got up and followed him.

While Jesus was having dinner at Matthew's house, many tax collectors and "sinners" came and ate with him and his disciples. When the Pharisees saw this, they asked his disciples, "Why does your teacher eat with tax collectors and 'sinners'?"

On hearing this, Jesus said, "It is not the healthy who need a doctor, but the sick. But go and learn what this means: 'I desire mercy, not sacrifice.' For I have not come to call the righteous, but sinners."[1]

—*Matthew the Tax Collector*

There was a fundamental incompatibility between the old Israel, paralyzed by self-righteousness and overloaded with petty regulations, and the new Israel humbled by the consciousness of sin, and turning in faith to Jesus the Messiah for forgiveness. The old garment could not contain the new cloth. The new wine of

messianic forgiveness could not be preserved in the parched wineskins of Jewish legalism.[2]
—R. V. G. Tasker

When the center of morality is avoidance—when virtue is a matter of continually whittling life down to proper size—it's all going to appear quite pale and stifling. If our primary focus is on remaining unspotted from the world, we'll invariably narrow our way down to pettiness in preserving our peculiar slice of religious turf undefiled. Evil seems all-encompassing, so our turning away becomes frantic flight. We must build ever higher, ever stricter barriers against the encroachment of the world. Morally safe activities steadily decrease; the true way of holiness steadily constricts.[3]
—Steven R. Mosley

Have you ever wrapped an empty box and given it to a friend as a gift? You bait them with comments. "I hope you like it." "I think it's perfect for you." Or, "I saved the receipt in case you need to exchange it."

You watch them open it—neatly at first, then more aggressively. They prepare to look pleased, politely intending to portray pleasure regardless of the contents. When they open the package, their confused facial expressions segue into laughter: "You got me this time." Unless you are completely coldhearted, you have the real present nearby.

I've reached many conclusions surveying the Invitations of Jesus. I feel that, in an innocent but dangerous sense, many Christians like me often wrap and distribute empty boxes to people craving real gifts. The packaging impresses. The presentation intrigues. We speak about the benefits and blessings of knowing Jesus. We build up expectations. We make promises. When the recipients open our packages, however, they often find them empty. If they do, we gave a false gospel; we shared a god other than the Jesus-God of Scripture.

This narrative of Matthew's call sheds light on the real Christ, on the real good news we desire to spread. Jesus came as a Friend to the friendless. The story is an Invitation proper: Jesus confronted another person one-on-one and issued a definitive statement of welcome. As with each Invitation, this one can affect how we experience Christ's call to us, and how we extend His call to others.

During my years of youth ministry, I often challenged teens to befriend classmates who had no friends. Driven by insecurities, their normal behavior consisted of frantic efforts to become popular with the popular, to become friends with those already bombarded with friends. Rather than expend such effort to join the "in crowd," I told them Christ would honor attempts at loving the "out crowd."

They could sit for lunch beside the boy everyone ignored. There was always an empty seat there. They could pick a kid for their team no one else would ever choose. It wouldn't take much work to give a smile, buy a soft drink or make a call to one of the many friendless faces they pass in the hallways. While I did not want them influenced negatively by the sin of classmates, they could make conscious efforts to see people as Jesus would.

How did He see them? How does He still see them? This narrative answers both questions.

As we study it, let's imagine we are watching a Power Point presentation of photos from events. All five slides are labeled. That title gives a descriptive caption of the scene. Watch closely. The drama accurately illustrates why Jesus came to earth. If you claim to follow Him and if we intend to lead others to join us, viewing the images in this scenario define the framework for our journey.

MATTHEW: RUNNING HIS BUSINESS

Few of us awake every morning eager to ask God's blessings on the Internal Revenue Service. Still, our feelings toward modern tax agents pale in comparison to the animosity people felt toward ancient collectors. During Christ's time they were a despised group. Haddon Robinson gives us a graphic sketch of the role Matthew and others like him played:

> "If you think this tax collector was merely a good-natured chap willing to admit his limitations, you do not understand the place of tax collectors in the first century. Whenever Rome wanted to tax a providence, it sold the right to tax to the highest bidder. And once a man purchased the right to tax, he was free to take anything the traffic would bear. He usually discovered it could bear a great deal. You couldn't do business without doing business with a tax collector. You couldn't move your goods from town to town without stopping by his desk.
>
> As a result, extortion was built into the job; injustice was a part of the trade. Tacitus, the Roman historian, says that once he visited a village that had such an honest tax collector that the village erected a monument to his memory. Some men are traitors by one craven deed of cowardice, but a tax collector was a traitor all day and every day. He was despised by most people. Instead, he spent much of his time with extortionists, evil doers, and the sexually loose."[4]

Jesus approached Matthew at his place of unethical and unpopular business. That greedy agent—despised and rejected by the religious, the wealthy, and the common—had no idea his routine would be interrupted. He didn't know his life was about to change. Jesus walked to the table where Matthew took advantage of anyone he could to obtain profit. Think of Jesus approaching that man in that place. It was like wearing a neon sign flashing, "I'll Be Friends With Anyone."

The scene fits fine with other callings in the Bible. For a person to be called at their place of employment appears to be a pattern. After blowing his first attempt at world changing, Moses capped a forty-year stay on the backside of the Midian desert watching his father-in-law's flocks. Then, a bush became ablaze. It turned out to be God calling him into the arena of leadership.

> A Friend to the Friendless

The young David was, as an afterthought, pulled in from shepherding to kingship. The giant killer, song writer, world changer, had no clue his journal entrees would still be sung around the world today.

Peter, Andrew, James and John received their call while hoping to haul in a decent meal. Matthew sat, running his business, when Jesus entered the stage.

Matthew never forgot it either. Later, when he listed his own name in the rundown of disciples, he identified himself as a tax collector.[5] Other gospel writers edited it out, maybe wanting "to forget that an apostle was engaged in his despised work, but Matthew himself never ceased to wonder that a social outcast such as himself should have been selected by Jesus for this high office."[6]

JESUS: RUINING HIS REPUTATION

Jesus was a terrible politician. He never played his cards right. This slide serves as a prime example of His political blundering. By approaching Matthew, Jesus raised the eyebrows of denominational executives. By speaking to Matthew, He gave them ammunition to use against Him. Then Jesus caused their ulcers to flare up when He invited Matthew to come along. But, like watering a lawn during a rainstorm, Jesus didn't stop.

He continued blowing His chance at religious and political stardom. He went home with Matthew and ate with him, sitting among the undesirables. Instead of working His way to the top of the Jewish establishment, instead of rubbing shoulders with the right people, Jesus palled with the wrong people. He entered the homes of the hated and saw them as important.

Again, Haddon Robinson eloquently presents the picture:

> "If Jesus appeared on earth today as He did 2000 years ago, many churches would not elect Him to their official boards. He would have disqualified Himself because He ran with the wrong crowd.
>
> The historian Luke comments that tax collectors and sinners—folks shunned by religious types because they made a

mess of life—kept seeking Him out to see what He had to say. When they came to Him Jesus gave a hearty welcome and often enjoyed dinner with them. Socializing with people like that ruined His testimony. The Pharisees and Bible teachers who observed Him wrote off His association with that element of society as a secret sympathy with sin. Yet, the fact remains. Jesus went out of His way to cultivate those relationships, and if we are serious about following Him, we must do the same thing."[7]

The purpose for Christ's coming was to look for and rescue the lost ones.[8] By fulfilling His reason for being He got into trouble. Did that bother Him? It doesn't look like it. Secure in God, He seemed unaffected by both praise and criticism. He didn't come to earth to build a reputation; in fact, involved in His incarnation was His status of having no reputation at all.[9]

We often go around ruining our reputations, also. We don't do it the way Christ did, though. It is usually immorality, arrogance, greed or stupidity that ruins reputations of people like us.

Why did Jesus lose all hope of winning a popularity contest? By loving people. How far we have fallen. We hobnob with the rich and religious to increase our resource pool, racing past the poor and hated as we rush. We build walls of separation around our church cliques while lonely neighbors bend ears of bartenders and mistresses—the only ones they find to listen.

Jesus built bridges. He beckoned all to come.

PHARISEES: REJECTING THE KINGDOM

The Pharisees have taken a bad rap, haven't they? We see them as resisters of Christ's revolution. We talk about them as if it was their creed to be as hypocritical as possible. This is incorrect. These were men sincerely wanting to serve Jehovah. They honestly thought they were succeeding. I complain about them and cut them down, failing to notice my reflection in their image.

More of Robinson's words assist us:

> "Measured by any conventional standard, ancient or modern, the Pharisee was a religious success. He says that he fasted twice a week. That was far more than the Old Testament had asked....He also says that he gave a tithe of all that he took in....
>
> The Pharisee was in deep earnestness about his religion; you had to be serious about it to make yourself as uncomfortable as he made himself. God was as real to him as the sheckles in his pocket, and he was willing to lower his standard of living a bit for him. And his religion had done him good: the people in his community respected and admired him as an outstanding citizen, a contributor to the community....
>
> If both of these men, the Pharisee and the tax collector, were running for political office, we would do our best to elect the Pharisee. If the tax collector got it, we would feel that corruption had invaded our society. If both of these men were courting your sister, you'd be pleased to have the Pharisee as brother-in-law, but hardly the tax collector."[10]

Why, then, the friction between Jesus and those religious conservatives? Jesus came preaching a universal sinfulness; they saw themselves as sinless. Because they observed both God-given and man-made laws of piety, they viewed themselves as several steps in front of the masses in a race toward God.

They played the game well. The trouble? They were playing the wrong game.

They were out of line because they focused on external conformity to rules rather than an internal character of righteousness.

From Moses' reception of the Law on Mount Sinai until Christ's time, the Jews had added rules and prohibitions. They turned requirements into a legal watchdog governing every deed. They drifted from pleasing God to taking pleasure in their upstanding positions. They set themselves up as moral conquerors of the ancient world. They were judges whose lives reflected criticism, not compassion.

Using the imagery of a dance, John Fischer shows how the freedom of Christ and the formalities of the Pharisees resulted in a serious tension.

"[Jesus] wanted to turn their empty religious movements into heartfelt, joyous dancing. He wanted them to exchange the grip of the Law for the freedom of the dance. But, they thought He was a clumsy dancer, always bumping into their traditions and stepping on their pious toes. He even danced with the wrong crowd in smokefilled rooms and on messy floors."[11]

By asking the disciples why Jesus associated with such "low life," the Pharisees proved how far they had fallen, even in spite of their belief in Jehovah. Like the Pharisees we should have high behavioral standards. We should shun sin and encourage others to do likewise. The Pharisees, however, rejected people, not just improper conduct. By demanding a certain performance level of themselves and others, they ended up rejecting the Messiah they had long awaited.

How sad. And what a warning to us. In our zeal for righteousness do we lean toward Pharisaism? In our efforts at purging society of sin do we push aside sinners? Have we elevated ourselves to a place of purity?

Yes, we often play the game well. But, are we playing the right game?

MATTHEW: RECEIVING THE KINGDOM

Matthew had very little in common with the Pharisees. When Jesus said, "Follow me," Matthew responded in such a way to further distance himself from them. They rejected the Kingdom; he eagerly embraced it. He got up and followed Jesus. In fact, Luke says Matthew "left everything and followed" Jesus.[12] He left behind his ticket to fortune.

What he lacked in popularity he had offset with a full pocketbook. His business was established. The Romans must have been pleased with his performance. We see no hint of an itch to change professions, a midlife crisis or his lean toward escapism. We simply see Christ's speaking two simple words and Matthew saying, "Yes." What a beautiful scene.

A Friend to the Friendless

Jesus made no promise of what life with Him would consist of. He did not hand Matthew a full color brochure. None of the other disciples were called forward to give glowing reports of how their pursuit of happiness ended when they found Jesus. Christ did not debate the pros and cons of being a tax collector, nor of being a Pharisee, nor of being a disciple.

What went through Matthew's mind? We can only speculate. So, let's do. He surely had to wonder why he jumped so suddenly from his way of life to follow a controversial Teacher. Was there something in the person of Jesus that drew Matthew? Christ did not resort to persuasive gimmicks; He only presented Himself as the drawing card for New Life.

Over the years we have missed the awesomeness of the Savior's call. Let's notice it now. It is simple, but life-changing. It is straightforward, but loving. The Invitation creates more questions than answers. Matthew's abruptness shocks us. It indicates that we often miss something in our response to Jesus.

While several chapters in this study underscore the necessity of careful evaluation, we must not lose sight of the truth we are being offered. Truth only a fool can refuse. Or, often, only a fool can accept.

Jesus' Invitation did not explain much to Matthew. Even the hush held a compelling beauty. Matthew's inevitable questions failed to blind him to that beauty. Our uncertainties often blind us, don't they? I need to learn from Matthew. The scene broadcasts truth I must notice: There is a time to throw Chris-caution to the wind to step into a place where Care is never lacking.

> "Where will our following take us, for instance? God only knows where it will take us, and we can be sure only that it will take us not where we want to go necessarily but where we are wanted, until, by a kind of alchemy, where we are wanted becomes where we want to go."[13]

Although Jesus didn't spell out the greatness of the Kingdom to lure Matthew toward it, on many occasions He presented the Kingdom as the most worthy of all worlds. To Jesus, Life in the

Kingdom is worth risking all else. Let's reread these words. Let's recapture the Kingdom vision Matthew caught a glimpse of through Christ.

> "The Kingdom of heaven is like a treasure hidden in a field. When a man found it, he hid it again, and then in his joy went and sold all he had and bought that field.
> Again, the Kingdom of heaven is like a merchant looking for fine pearls. When he found one of great value, he went away and sold everything he had and bought it."[14]

We live in a culture where Christians want to blend their Christianity in with all we are and all we do. Jesus presented the Kingdom as a New Life, not a new list or a new twist or a new flavor. Matthew saw that New Life partially. But, his glimpse of Life in the face of Jesus propelled him to rid himself of all in order to purchase the Real Field.

GOD: RECONCILING MEN UNTO HIMSELF

This slide is a wide angle shot of the entire scene. All that takes place in this story has a purpose larger than what is visible. God orchestrated the events. He worked in His Son to reconcile humans unto Himself.[15] For that reason Christ never wavered when confronted with His reason for being: "I have not come to call the righteous, but sinners."[16] Through Christ God removed the dividing wall of sin and joined hands with all who leave their tables to follow Him.

> "In Christianity God is the great and merciful Initiator. He reaches down to needy humanity. In all other religions of the world humans reach up in search of reality and salvation. The 'but God' rings through apostolic preaching. God broke through and entered history: He loved the world; He acted in the interests of the world; He sent His Son to procure salvation."[17]

God is the subject of these invitational dramas. We are the objects. He loves. He forgives. He heals. We receive His love. We are made clean. We become whole.

Modern messages often place us at the center of the drama. Biblically, God's work must be the focus. The cross, signifying God's act of ultimate love, stands at the center as a haunting reminder of the One who came to be a Friend to the friendless.

He called sinners. Called? That words means to Invite "as one would a guest to dinner."[18] At our tables Christ comes without regard for His reputation. He comes to our tables of religiosity, sin, frustration, addiction, apathy—and He hopes to reconcile us to God.

Will we remain at our tables or follow Him? Matthew rose from his tables of habit and security. He received the Kingdom. The Pharisees sat glued to their tables of originally sincere, but then self-serving religion. They rejected the Kingdom.

"Get up from your table," Messiah still says. "Come to mine. At my table I offer bread and wine as proof of my eternal Friendship. At my table I have a place for you. Won't you come?"

REJOICE that this ministry helps share the Invitation: This story first appeared in Charisma magazine. Taking risks many readers might question, Charisma has been diving into the lost world to find ways to reach them. Do not rebuke a magazine for sending Invitations. Charisma is a monthly magazine designed to inform people about how God is working in the world today through His Holy Spirit. It includes testimonies, commentary about current culture and news from many nations of the world. www.charismamag.com

RELEASE your worries by praying, "God, give me strength to break open the walls of separation."

RECEIVE Christ's Invitation by spending time with someone few others care for.

RESPOND by Inviting a friend the way Jesus would. Who will you Invite?

RENEW your mind by reading books by John Fischer and Bob Briner.

Chapter 7

LIFE AFTER DEATH

While Jesus was still speaking, some men came from the house of Jairus, the synagogue ruler. "Your daughter is dead," they said. "Why bother the teacher any more?"

Ignoring what they said, Jesus told the synagogue ruler, "Don't be afraid; just believe."

He did not let anyone follow him except Peter, James and John the brother of James. When they came to the home of the synagogue ruler, Jesus saw a commotion, with people crying and wailing loudly. He went in and said to them, "Why all this commotion and wailing? The child is not dead but asleep." But they laughed at him.

After he put them all out, he took the child's father and mother and the disciples who were with him, and went in where the child was. He took her by the hand and said to her, "Talitha koum!" (which means, "Little girl, I say to you, get up!"). Immediately the girl stood up and walked around (she was twelve years old). At this they were completely astonished. He gave strict orders not to let anyone know about this, and told them to give her something to eat.[1]

—Mark

"What would you like to be when you grow up little girl?"
"Alive."[2]

—Calvin Miller

God does not expect us to submit our faith to him without reason, but the very limits of our reason make faith a necessity.[3]

—Augustine

Death. The word sounds cold, final. Attempts to calm its sting by substituting euphemisms like "passed away" only veil reality without altering it. Critics contend that man has invented religion to ease the pain of death. We all wonder what life is like beyond death, or if there is any life there at all. One fact is certain: the creature of death looms ominously in the distance. It's ready to disarm our feeble attempts at good health, safety and longevity.

Some people claim to have returned back to life after dying. They testify of various types of "out of body" experiences. Long tunnels. Bright lights. Grassy fields. Blended voices. Familiar faces. Listeners hear them and feel amazed while asking, "Did they actually leave life then return?" "Were they hallucinating?" "Are facts as convincing as these stories sound?"

I like hearing the stories but I, of course, don't know. I've almost died, but I remember doctors and nurses and tests and tears and hooked machines. Not mass choirs or golden gates. I can, however, look to the future and not fear, despite death's threatening presence. My hope lies in the victory won by Christ. Scripture claims He conquered death. By entering the mouth of death Jesus removed its venom. Yes, death still awaits. But it doesn't have the last word.

The season of spring celebrates life bursting forth from death. Bright flowers and green leaves remind us of a return, an arrival, a resurrection, a life. Christianity claims Jesus died and rose again. And that He invites observers to share in His conquest. As Victor, Christ gives life for the living and the dying.

This Invitation shows His mastery over that seemingly invincible foe. During His life and death, enemies couldn't block His path. They tried. They failed. Again He spoke tender words of Invitation: "Little girl, I say to you, get up!" We witness Jesus going about His Father's business. Let's eavesdrop on the story, noticing the working principles. Maybe they can also work in our situations.

PRESENCE FOR THE ANXIOUS

In Chapter 5 we learned that Jesus first ministers with His presence. Notice the word "presence," not "presents." Too often we attempt to reduce the Lord of Glory to a Santa Clause distributing bags of goodies to us, His good little boys and girls. Verse 24 says Jesus "went with him." As His first response to this urgent need, Jesus gave Himself to this distressed father. As this man's daughter moved closer to death, he needed something. He received Someone. Jesus brought no facts or formulas, no songs or sermons. He brought no promise. Only His presence.

He comes to us like that, too, doesn't He? We desperately need to learn we need the Healer more than we need healing; we need the Giver more than we need His gifts. Scripture highlights this by labeling the Holy Spirit as "the Comforter." The Spirit is the one called along beside us. Into the anxious, fearful moments of our lives, He graces us by giving us Himself. Whatever the situation. He is with us always, even to the end of the age, to the end of our strength, to the end of our sanity.[4]

What would happen if we focused on Him when we became anxious? Not an attempt to "fake it 'till we make it." Not pretending to be composed when inner and outer worlds explode. We can honestly face anxiety. But it only works when we know Christ has entered the problem with us. He gives us Himself.

As I state repeatedly, these Invitations of Jesus can show us not only how He invites us, but also how we can invite others. Learning from Christ's practice of ministry by presence we can, as Christ's ambassadors, minister to others by being with them. Four principles will enable us to more effectively share His presence with the anxious:

1. LISTEN: Stop preaching long enough to hear what the hurt ones are saying.
2. LEARN: Often we assume too much. Learn from those who are needy. A humble person is willing to learn.
3. LOVE: Do we love others or see them as pawns in our religious games? People aren't numbers or opportunities to expand our ministries; they are individuals loved immensely by an awesome God. Join Him. Love them.
4. LOOK: Enter their pain with them. Then connect as they search for the Presence. Maybe they'll believe Christ is there. Maybe they won't miss Him. Don't just look at them. Look with them.

These four words can guide us in reaching others. Let's allow this statement to echo in our minds and encourage our actions: Never bombard people with the principles of Christianity without first blessing them with the Presence of Christ.

BELIEF FOR THE FEARFUL

Verse 36 records Christ's statement to a shocked and saddened father who has just been told his daughter died. Jesus says, "Don't be afraid. Just believe." After offering His presence for the anxious one, Jesus offered faith for the fearful. Jesus did not promote a simplistic foolishness that avoided the problem. He suggested a simple faith that could overcome the problem.

Jesus frequently urged people to possess faith. He often rebuked the disciples for their lack of it. In the parenthetical story sandwiched inside this narrative, Jesus proclaims that faith saved the woman with the issue of blood.[5] Here He encouraged a devastated synagogue ruler to have faith, to believe.

Why did Jesus recommend faith over fear? Fear blinds and restricts. Faith hopes. It is the substance of what is hoped for and the proof of what can't be noticed.[6] Seeing isn't believing. Believing is seeing. Belief is the opposite of pessimism, which sees reality and gives up because the odds appear too great. Belief compares the odds to God.

Faith isn't presumption. Presumption assumes God will do what we want Him to because we incorrectly think He owes us a favor. Belief differs greatly from that and it makes two significant assumptions:

1. God possesses the knowledge of what would be best in any given situation.
2. God possesses the power to carry out that which He knows is best.

Modern merchandisers of the gospel have adulterated the concept of faith. Reducing the living faith Christ taught to a mechanical formula for obtaining personal cravings, these shallow self-servers distort a glorious reality. In hearing Jesus tell Jairus to believe, think of the faith of Scripture. Not ministry magic from evangelistic "t.v.ology."

Faith shouldn't be associated with escapism either. Such a slant sees problems then denies their existence. When surface denial fails, escapists turn to chemicals or experiences that momentarily numb their pain. Christians might choose religious methods of escaping. But their pseudo-coping must not be confused with faith. Faith never closes its eyes to see reality. It doesn't see less than what is really there. It sees more. Much more.

Cowards run. Critics complain. Christians believe. The heroes of Scripture are not the beautiful ones but the believing ones. They aren't the ones who never failed, but the fallen who race or rumble back by faith. Possessing such faith is more possible when we trust the character of the object of our belief.

Jairus had heard and seen what Jesus could do. Then he was told to believe. The pages of Scripture, history and personal experience resound with the ample proof of God's power. Evidence exists. Can we join Jairus and believe? In bad situations can we make a trade, opting for faith instead of fear?

TRUTH FOR THE MOURNERS

When the ancient eastern people mourned, they held back nothing. They wailed. They voiced hurt. They cried with tears, groans, songs. Grief was a public event. Sounds of their sadness spilled into city streets. Christ walked into such a beehive of mourning and said, "The child is not dead but asleep."

While the family and hired mourners wailed in consternation, Christ walked in with confidence, with calmness. Sounds strange, doesn't it? Either He didn't care much or He knew much more. He seemed insensitive but the Bible abounds with proof of His compassion. Yes, Jesus cared for the young girl. His composure stemmed from the fact that He knew what the others didn't. Because of that, He offered Truth to the mourners.

Suppose a driver knew a red light meant stop. The driver didn't know, though, that if the red light was blinking he could proceed if the road was clear. So he stopped. And remained stopped though the sign gave permission to go. The line of cars behind him grew longer. The coast was clear, yet he didn't move on because he acted on the truth he knew. He knew truth (red = stop). Just not the whole truth (blinking red = stop, look, proceed when clear). That man's correct knowledge needed more knowledge. I'm sure someone eventually informed the driver of the blinking red light's true meaning. The words they used just can't be used here.

Similarly, the mourners saw death as the end. They based behavior on truth known. Jesus knew more. The cessation of a heartbeat wasn't the story's conclusion. Jesus knew that.

Truth is the dimension of life that, once we grasp it, can set us free. Bound by their limited knowledge of life and death, the grieving group needed Truth for freedom. Jesus told them the truth regarding the little girl's condition. Evidence indicated an end. Jesus knew the whole truth.

By telling them what they didn't know, Jesus replaced the music of mourning with the tune of Truth. I remember when I attended college and worked as a DJ on a country music station. I occasionally broke rules and played an uplifting Christian song. Nothing against country music lovers. You must confess, though, that many are depressing. A steady diet of broken hearts and bar stools? I decided a few songs of joy served as a good medicine.

Into the depression of the characters in our story, Jesus sang the great news of Truth. To the family, His good words voiced hope. To the designated wailers, His words ruined a great day of gloom. To us He can do the same. Let Him speak, sing and breathe truth. Into our pain, He brings Himself. He asks us to believe. Then He tells us the rest of the story.

LIFE FOR THE DEAD

Often, many over-zealous hyper-faith types err here. They exalt the benefits of faith. They promise a healing. If no healing comes, they blame lack of faith or funds. Actually, the healer may have acted on desire rather than Truth. Jesus was different. He knew the girl would live beyond her death. Therefore He could, and did, deliver her. The Master Invited her to arise. And she did.

Was she really dead? Yes. Luke says, "Her spirit returned."[7] As a doctor, Luke would not make that statement lightly. This story illustrates God's love and His power.

"Man's despair was God's opportunity. Christ had already been shown as Lord of nature; it was necessary that He be shown as Lord of life....It was extremely fitting that He, who created life first, before sin and death entered the world, should show Himself now as the Master of death and the grave. More, this was an important piece of preliminary evidence for His own resurrection: He who could conquer death in others could burst bonds Himself. The central miracle of the Bible is ever resurrection, because it must be the central fact of all true Christian experience."[8]

Jesus invited her. She came. To life. To Him.

If He can give life to the dead, can't He give life to the deceived, the depressed, the defeated, the doubting? As Lord of Life He allows no grave, no experience, no situation to bind us when He says, "Come forth." He doesn't always bring the dead to life. But He always gives Life—abundant Life—before, during and after any death or any disaster. He is the Lord of Life.

INSTRUCTIONS FOR THE ASTONISHED

Our last point would have been the perfect conclusion. A dead girl came back to life. The family rejoiced. An audience turned mourning into dancing. Three cheers for Jesus! But Christ didn't end it there. As we often see in His Invitations, Jesus threw in an unexpected twist. This story ended with Jesus pronouncing an unusual benediction: "He gave strict orders not to let anyone know about this, and told them to give her something to eat."[9]

While an astonished crowd watched, Christ resisted the opportunity to become a spectacle or a sideshow. I want a shout here, a song there, and a business meeting agenda nearby. Jesus—as He often did—discouraged talk about His miracles. No ads, front-page photos, film series. No convention, promotion, news flash. Maybe He knew the effect it would have on His ministry, on His followers, on His future.

Sure it would have been a drawing card. But the emphasis would have been misplaced. He was more concerned with how much ministry took place than how marketable He became. Though a crowd had been with Him, He only took the girl's parents and His three closest friends back with Him for the encounter. Throughout His life, Jesus met needs but refused to be just another medicine man.

Would I attempt to keep quiet after such a miracle? I know me. I also wonder about modern miracle makers who refuse to pray for the sick in hospitals or slums. In their conferences, in their atmosphere, in their control—they pray. Especially if the cameras are rolling. Surely their hearts are right. But surely Jesus would race toward other little girls in far away places and bring Life. His conclusion might tell His co-workers to remain silent.

Jesus dealt with practical things. Think of Him rounding up a peanut better and jelly sandwich for the revived girl. Jesus met needs. He didn't advertise. Jesus built the Kingdom, not an image or an empire the human way.

Us? Noticing Christ's miracles merging with His refusal to posture for popularity, I need to learn from Him.

- To the anxious, Jesus said, "I will never leave you or forsake you."[10]

- To the fearful, Jesus said, "Blessed are those who have not seen and yet believe."[11]
- To the mourners, Jesus said, "My ways are not your ways. You see through the glass darkly, but I know something you don't."[12]
- To the dying Jesus said, "I am the Resurrection and the Life."[13]
- To the astonished, Jesus said, "Marvel not that the demons are subject to you, but rejoice if your names are written in the Lamb's book of Life.[14]

Maybe that is a nice way to end. Thinking of our names there. Thinking of Christ's Invitations, of His words and miracles luring us and our friends there. Thinking not only of death, but also of resurrection. Maybe we will see Jairus and His daughter. Maybe we will see Peter, James and John. Maybe we will see the woman with an issue of blood. And maybe we will see Jesus, that Great Inviter, Surpriser, Defeater of Death.

His Life gave proof: death is no match for Him.

REJOICE that this ministry helps share the Invitation: I often teach these Invitations to Youth With a Mission students. Youth With A Mission (YWAM) is an international missions organization committed to fulfilling Christ's Great Commission to "Go into all the world and preach the Gospel to all creation." (Mark 16:15) YWAM was founded in 1960 by Loren Cunningham and since that time thousands have served in every country of the world. They use three methods of action to take the gospel to the world: Evangelism (spreading God's message), Training (preparing workers to reach others), Mercy Ministries (showing God's love through practical assistance). YWAM Orlando, like all of YWAM, is committed to Know God and Make Him known. There are over a billion people who have never heard the name of Jesus. So, YWAM is committed to recruit, prepare and send laborers and leaders to reach these unreached with the gospel of Christ. The Orlando campus holds various training schools (courses) like the Discipleship Training School. Each course receives credit with the University of the Nations. They also offer opportunities to reach out through Global Outreach Teams, King's Kids (a program for youth ages 8 to 18) and Mission Adventures (a program for Junior and Senior High youth groups as well as college and career groups). www.ywamorlando.org.

RELEASE your worries by praying, "God, let me have new faith to see what my eyes can't notice."

RECEIVE Christ's Invitation by letting Him bring new life to you, to a family, to a friend.

RESPOND by Inviting a friend the way Jesus would. Who will you Invite?

RENEW your mind by reading books by Eugene Peterson, Max Lucado, Scott Hagan, Doug Beacham, and Cec Murphy.

Chapter 8

COMING TO CHRIST FOR THE REST OF YOUR LIFE

Come to me, all you who are weary and burdened, and I will give you rest. Take my yoke upon you and learn from me, for I am gentle and humble in heart, and you will find rest for your souls. For my yoke is easy and my burden is light.[1]

—Jesus

It is an old and ironic habit of human beings to run faster when we have lost our way.[2]

—Rollo May

Instead of trusting in a God who is predictable in His steadfastness and reliable in His faithfulness, many Christians are filled with fears and anxiety because at a deep gut-level they sense God to be untrustworthy.[3]

—David Seamands

Come to Jesus for the rest of your life. That statement, very compatible with the theme of this study, appears to offer an easily understandable invitation. It seems to say, "Come to Christ and never leave," encouraging the reader to draw near to Christ permanently. Although I hope Christ's Invitations present that message, the statement actually emphasizes something different. Read it again. Interpret the word "rest" to mean "peace" or "relief," rather than "remainder" or "entirety."

Come to Jesus for rest and peace and relief in life. Jesus originally spoke these words to a culture much different from ours. But, like us, I am sure the original hearers struggled with properly prioritizing their lives.

Undoubtedly they confused wants and needs. Surely the vanity of the temporal frequently blinded them. Though different, they needed the invitation just as we do.

And we most certainly need it. We are a busy, burdened people. Agrarian societies worked very hard for long hours to provide the necessities of life. They would end days worn out, while we are more frequently stressed out. In our technological, information oriented world we are not over-worked, but over-rushed. Like hamsters on a wheel, we go nowhere fast, burdened by the pressure to get there quickly. We hurry to arrive nowhere well-dressed, well-loved and wealthy. We assume we will be happy upon arrival, but that day never comes. What a rapid ride it is, this human race.

We suffer in countless ways. We cry out for relief. When physically exhausted from hard labor or hurried leisure, we sink into a recliner for relaxation. When mentally drained, we put our brains in neutral. When emotionally spent, we seek an escape.

Fortunately, Jesus did not come to exclusively recruit the healthy and whole. He invited, and invites, the hurting. That's us. Let's examine the invitation and praise God that Christ calls tired ones to Himself and offers deep, true, peaceful rest.

THE INVITER: JESUS

In weeks preceding election, we receive a barrage of political propaganda. Each candidate presents promises to attract voters and personal qualifications to impress them. The list of achievements and hobbies convey the message that the man or woman is regular enough to represent us, but unique enough to lead us.

This invitation includes a personal bio of Jesus. Instead of presenting only a promise, He spoke of Himself. Jesus told listeners more than the "what" of His welcome; He revealed facts of Himself, the "who." The qualifications that accompanied His words of welcome let us know who He is and why He has the right to extend such an attractive offer.

He said He was gentle and humble. How drastically different from qualities expected of contemporary leaders. Experts instruct us that a leader must be self-assertive, confident, demanding and direct. Though Jesus exhibited many characteristics we would consider compatible with today's leadership models, He surprises us with the two traits listed on His resume. Gentleness and humility seem out of character for a king, especially the King of an eternal kingdom.

To be gentle is to be considerate, meek and unassuming.[4] Such qualities score few points on the modern management meter. We look for the driven ones, even if their driving takes them over the backs of others. If they are determined to make it to the top, we want them on our team. Jesus said, "I am gentle." The contrast is striking.

Humility means choosing to take the low road, refusing to promote self. The same word speaks of mountains and hills made low. Many leaders are anthills trying to act like mountains. Jesus, in such a different manner, lived as a mountain willingly made low to reach those dwelling at the bottom.[5]

This week I heard of an evangelist offering life-sized posters of himself to those who donate funds to his television enterprise. Compare that with Christ. I really don't expect the corporate world to commend the virtues of gentleness and humility, but the Christian world should. Our identity comes from One who described Himself with those two words: gentle, humble. Yet, His followers? We often describe ourselves as "internationally known" and "truly anointed." Again, the contrast is striking.

Jesus elaborated further on Himself and promised that His yoke is easy, His burden is light. Most of us have seen, at least in photographs, oxen wearing yokes. The frame joins the animals, allowing them to work together pulling a plow. In New Testament times the restrictive nature of the law caused many to refer to it as a yoke.[6] Jesus warned the experts of the law, saying, "Woe to you experts in the law because you load people down with burdens they can hardly carry and you yourselves will not lift one finger to help them."[7]

Jesus admitted He has a yoke to offer. Unlike the Pharisees, His yoke is easy, His burden is light. An easy yoke is one that fits properly, is suitable, good and useful.[8] A light burden weighs little.

So Jesus, the Master Inviter, described Himself as a gentle, humble man who has for His followers a properly fitting yoke and an easy to carry burden.

THE INVITED: WEARY ONES

After revealing His qualifications as the Inviter, Jesus told who He welcomes. The address label on the Invitation reads: "to the weary and burdened." "Weary" speaks of tiredness or exhaustion.[9] John used the word to describe Jesus' condition after a long journey.[10] "Burdened" refers to those carrying something and is a form of the word Jesus used to describe Himself as the One offering a light burden.[11]

The traditional wording of this verse, "those who labor and are heavy laden,"[12] paints an accurate picture of Christ's intent. The invitation goes out to those who labor in the service of formal religion, or those who labor to serve, satisfy or justify themselves. There are many types of labor that place us in the position to be qualified for this invitation. Think of your life and your labors. In what ways are you burdened?

- Religious activity
- Sinful habits
- Self-hate

- Depression
- Guilt
- Fear
- Loneliness
- Chemical dependence
- Spiritual confusion

The list could go on. Whatever the source of weariness, an Invitation has been spoken by the gentle and humble Savior. He can alleviate the crushing load of guilt. He can calm the storm of fear. He can free us from the prison of habit. Weary? Burdened? This message, this Messiah, is for us.

Charles Swindoll sums up the condition of the weary ones:

> "Lots of things are fine in themselves, but our strength has its limits...and before long fatigue cuts our feet out from beneath us. The longer the weariness lingers, the more we face the danger of that weary condition clutching our inner man by the throat and strangling our hope, our motivation, our spark, our optimism, our encouragement."[13]

Sound familiar? Let's continue on and see the glorious promise encased inside this comforting Invitation.

THE INVITATION: COME AND RECEIVE REST

Christ told the weary to come. He knows who He is and what He can do for us. Yet, He refuses to force Himself upon us. His meekness is evident; during His years here He never resorted to any high-pressure salesmanship. The offer He presented is the world's best opportunity, but He merely spoke it in kind, straight-forward terms and left decisions to hearers.

Then, He explained what to do once we come to Him. We are to take upon ourselves His yoke. We are to learn of Him. Coming to Christ involves submitting to His life-view. It means entering into relationship with Him.

Only as we accept the yoke can we truly know that it fits. Only as we learn of Jesus can we be touched by His gentleness and humility.

He did not suggest a casual glance from afar. Many take such a look, then assume they are in Christ. The distance of separation, though, is large. A look at the Invitations of Jesus reveals that coming to Him involves a rational, but also a radical decision. That settlement unites us with our Maker. Observation is not enough. Coming leads to abiding.

Jesus clearly stated the results of such a decision. The one who comes to Christ will find rest. What is the process of the distribution of rest? Jesus gives it as a gift, only available through the Giver. Our responsibility is to come. He provides the gift of rest.

Another fact is interesting to notice. Usually, when weary, we look for rest. We search for a peace that persistently eludes us. But, we continue searching in hopes that our fate will change.

Jesus does not tell us to halt our pursuit. He suggests another, much more worthy object of that pursuit: Himself. By frantically chasing peace and happiness, we distance ourselves even farther from them. Seeking Christ, on the other hand, means coming to One who possesses a peace unmatched elsewhere.[14] So, rest is the by-product of communion with Christ.

Larry Crabb beautifully describes this concept:

> "Now there is nothing wrong in wanting to be happy. An obsessive preoccupation with 'my happiness,' however, often obscures our understanding of the biblical route to deep, abiding joy. The Lord has told us that there are pleasures at His right hand. If we desire pleasures, we must learn what it means to be at God's right hand. Paul tells us that Christ has been exalted to God's right hand (Ephesians 1:20). It follows naturally that the more I abide in Christ, the more I will enjoy the pleasure available in fellowship with God. If I am to experience true happiness, I must desire above all else to become more like the Lord, to live in subjection to the Father's will as He did."[15]

Once again, Charles Swindoll amplifies this for us:

"But let's understand that God does not dispense strength and encouragement like a druggist fills your prescription. The Lord doesn't promise to give us something to take so we can handle our weary moments. He promises us Himself. That is all. And that is enough....In place of our exhaustion and spiritual fatigue, He will give us rest. All that He asks is that we come to Him...that we spend a little while thinking about Him, meditating on Him, talking to Him, listening in silence, occupying ourselves with Him—totally and thoroughly lost in the hiding place of His presence."[16]

I wrote much of this chapter during a short missionary trip. Watching as primitive Indians labored arduously to provide the basics of life, I remembered that it was a similar society hearing these words when Jesus spoke them. Extreme physical work was the routine.

Christ spoke to them with words of encouragement. He offered hope of a better day, a more restful day.

Surely any audience would be drawn to this message. The original listeners needed it. We need it. Those near us need it.

The words of the Invitation are lovely. They have been read, quoted and expounded upon so many times. But, Jesus intended that they change our lives, not hang on our walls.

Let's hear His Invitation. Let's hit the altar and find rest. We will then be altered for the rest of our lives.

REJOICE that this ministry helps share the Invitation: This chapter first appeared as an article in Today's Pentecostal Evangel. As the official weekly magazine of the U.S. Assemblies of God, it provides the non-Christian with the good news of salvation through Jesus Christ while encouraging believers to pursue a deeper walk with God through the work of the Holy Spirit. The Evangel offers inspirational features that center on contemporary issues in addition to relevant news, biblical instruction, devotional guides and interviews with Christian leaders. Typically, the Evangel focuses on such topics as marriage and family, sanctity of life, finances, health, social issues and events that have shaped Christianity. Also regularly featured is the domestic and international missions work of the Assemblies of God. The Evangel has a weekly audience of at least 250,000 readers. www.pe.ag.org

RELEASE your worries by praying, "God, give me peace today."

RECEIVE Christ's Invitation by taking a prayer walk as a way of leaving the pressure and receiving His peace.

RESPOND by Inviting a friend the way Jesus would. Who will you Invite?

RENEW your mind by reading books to help make your pace and your peace more stable. Books by Richard Foster, Dallas Willard, and John Ortberg will help.

Chapter 9

THIRSTY FOR LOVE

Now he had to go through Samaria. So he came to a town in Samaria called Sychar, near the plot of ground Jacob had given to his son Joseph. Jacob's well was there, and Jesus, tired as he was from the journey, sat down by the well. It was about the sixth hour.

When a Samaritan woman came to draw water, Jesus said to her, "Will you give me a drink?" (His disciples had gone into the town to buy food.)

The Samaritan woman said to him, "You are a Jew and I am a Samaritan woman. How can you ask me for a drink?" (For Jews do not associate with Samaritans.)

Jesus answered her, "If you knew the gift of God and who it is that asks you for a drink, you would have asked him and he would have given you living water."

"Sir," the woman said, "you have nothing to draw with and the well is deep. Where can you get this living water? Are you greater than our father Jacob, who gave us the well and drank from it himself, as did also his sons and his flocks and herds?"

Jesus answered, "Everyone who drinks this water will be thirsty again, but whoever drinks the water I give him will never thirst. Indeed, the water I give him will become in him a spring of water welling up to eternal life."

The woman said to him, "Sir, give me this water so that I won't get thirsty and have to keep coming here to draw water."

He told her, "Go, call your husband and come back."

"I have no husband," she replied.

Jesus said to her, "You are right when you say you have no husband. The fact is, you have had five husbands, and the man you now have is not your husband. What you have just said is quite true."

"Sir," the woman said, "I can see that you are a prophet. Our fathers worshiped on this mountain, but you Jews claim that the place where we must worship is in Jerusalem."

Jesus declared, "Believe me, woman, a time is coming when you will worship the Father neither on this mountain nor in Jerusalem. You Samaritans worship what you do not know; we worship what we do know, for salvation is from the Jews. Yet a time is coming and has now come when the true worshipers will worship the Father in spirit and truth, for they are the kind of worshipers the Father seeks. God is spirit, and his worshipers must worship in spirit and in truth."

The woman said, "I know that Messiah" (called Christ) "is coming. When he comes, he will explain everything to us."

Then Jesus declared, "I who speak to you am he."[1]

—St. John

The throat of our soul is parched, thirsty for the water of loving relationship and meaningful personal satisfaction.[2]

—Larry Crabb

We know that we desire happiness, purpose and love. Yet the simplest desires seem to be beyond our reach. Is there anyone who has identified what blocks us from what we seek but cannot find?[3]

—Rebecca Manley Pippert

My friend and I browsed through a Barnes & Noble bookstore. I struck up a conversation with the store manager. He seemed friendly and eager to know more about us. Halfway through our conversation I told him we were both pastors.

He was shocked. Not because he doesn't like ministers, but because he'd never really had a decent conversation with a Christian. "I normally only hear from Christians when they are mad," he told us.

The three of us sat down at the coffee bar. The manager told tales about religious people who had called, written or walked in his store to inform him they would never do business with him because of objectionable books or Halloween displays.

The man thanked us for being different and then excused himself so he could get back to work. My thoughts were racing so fast I found it hard to finish my bagel. No best seller could have taught us what we learned from that honest man.

I asked my friend, and myself, "How can believers shine a light and promote the gospel in a sinful, wicked world?" Maybe God wants people today to follow the example of Jesus. Time and technology have changed, but yesterday's techniques can still touch today's world.

Sitting idly as silent witnesses isn't enough. Lumbering ahead to peddle words without the Spirit is too much. We need to reach the world as Jesus did. He models a personal, realistic approach to speaking forth the good news. Let's stare at Him again. Let's discover the steps Christ used to initiate conversation with the people He met and open the door for true evangelism.

JESUS BROKE THE RULES

Alone and worn from His journey, Jesus sat by a well. His robe flashed no religious logo.

A woman approached to draw water.

The middle of the day was a strange time for her to undertake this task. People habitually took care of such business before the sun became their enemy. Gathering in the morning or evening hours made the climate work in their favor, as labor turned into an arena for conversation. They socialized as they worked.

Not that woman. She came during the heat of the day, revealing her standing with society. Enduring the relentless afternoon sun was better than suffering the silence of a condemning group gathered around a well.

Jesus was not put off by her presence. In fact, His choosing to not leave when she drew near underscored the first dynamic of evangelism illustrated by this story: Jesus broke the rules.

Devout Jews despised the people of Samaria. Jesus didn't. He refused to allow man's religious rules to hinder His purpose. Travel through a sinful city? Converse with a woman? A Samaritan woman? A Samaritan woman known for her wicked ways? Such acts were never done.

Except by Jesus. He came to do the will of His Father without concern for religious or social tradition. Children, sinners, prostitutes, thieves, poor, uneducated people—He touched all those ignored by religious rule-keepers.

The clean hands of strict legalists would not dare applaud His efforts. But He continued. And He reminded listeners of His purpose: "It is not the healthy who need a doctor, but the sick. I have not come to call the righteous, but sinners to repentance."[4]

Jesus remained on course despite strong winds of Pharisaical opposition that sought to blow Him in another direction. He broke rules; they judged Him guilty by association. Their muttering confirmed that He remained true to His agenda: "This man welcomes sinners and eats with them."[5]

Eating with people during Christ's day carried social significance. Christ embraced people others avoided. He associated with the guilty to reach them, not to become like them. But in order to reach them, He first entered their world.

Years later, Paul would keep Christ's rule-breaking trend moving forward. This is why:

"Though I am free and belong to no man, I make myself a slave to everyone, to win as many as possible. To the Jews I became like a Jew, to win the Jews. To those under the law I became like one under the law (though I myself am not under the law), so as to win those under the law. To those not having the law I became like one not having the law (though I am not free from God's law but am under Christ's law), so as to win those not having the law. To the weak I became weak, to win the weak. I have become all things to all men so that by all possible means I might save some. I do all this for the sake of the gospel, that I may share in its blessings."[6]

Let's learn. Let's not become more comfortable criticizing sinners than converting them. The color of a person's skin or the habits of a person's life must never prohibit us from reaching out to them. It is imperative that we welcome all.

Jesus allowed the woman to approach. Then He initiated conversation.

JESUS BROKE THE ICE

We often wonder how to begin a discussion with an unbeliever or how to channel dialogue toward the gospel. It is awkward making the transition from career questions or weather expectations to spiritual realities. But the Holy Spirit possesses an amazing ability to steer conversations toward eternal matters if we flow with Him.

We say we believe that people without Christ lack what can help them the most. Yet many times we speak as salesmen not sold on our own product. Jesus talked, listened and observed. He found common ground.

Thirsty beside a well, He asked the woman for water. She had the power to give it. What a wonderful way to break the ice, guiding the discussion in a good direction. The right words at the right time can open doors of great opportunity.[7]

Jesus did not use the same phrases every time He reached out to someone. He observed a situation and spoke words that moved toward truth. Now that task is our role, our calling.

Often, as we seek to reach out, our behavior will break the ice better than our conversation. Actions of love do speak louder than words.

Years ago a storm hit hard in southern Mexico. The dangerous weather washed out a bridge necessary for travel between two key cities. Hoping to quickly solve their problem, a large group gathered for a night of hurried repair.

Larry Myers, of Mexico Ministries, had labored among those people, but had struggled to build good rapport with them. Though he had previously planted churches in hundreds of Mexican communities, at that place he found spiritual resistance.

He prayed. He hoped. He wondered how to reach the people. Then he saw that their problem provided an opportunity to break the ice.

As men toiled, Myers purchased a truckload of tacos and drove to the work site. When he arrived, he provided food and assisted their labor. His act of kindness broke the ice in a town that now serves as a key location for his national outreach. A church. A school. A hospital. As a result of his involvement, the city shifted in a positive spiritual direction.

JESUS BROKE THE NEWS

What purpose would we serve by gaining friends and never telling them what we believe is the best news of all? Lifestyle witnessing opens the door to evangelism, but eventually we must verbalize the Story.

Jesus perceived that the Samaritan woman was thirsty for more than a drink of water. Her shifts from man to man indicated a craving for acceptance that eluded surface relationships. Jesus did not preach. He probed.

He went "beyond the externals to the heart of the problem—in this case an inability to be committed to one person for any length of time. So the drabness and apparent uselessness of her life is pierced by Jesus' insight and this opens the way for a new set of values and a new way of life and of looking at herself."[8]

I learned during my teen years how important it is to bring the good news to others; an experience I had with a friend convinced

Thirsty for Love

me I needed to be more aggressive in voicing my beliefs. We both played as point guards on our high school basketball team. My friend was two years older. I hoped to take his place as a team leader when he graduated.

Before then, though, he heard the gospel. He shared his experience with me, concluding his testimony with a smile. But, as I walked off with him, the expression on his face changed to a real concern. He Invited me to follow Jesus.

When I told him I already was following Jesus, he stopped walking. Staring at me, he asked, "If you have been a Christian all this time, why did you never tell me I needed to become one?"

His question pricked me. If I truly believed what I thought I believed, why had I talked with him about everything—sports, music, girls, family, school—except what mattered most?

Was I ashamed?[9]

My attitude changed. I began to witness to classmates, teammates and strangers. I spoke about the gospel, taught about it, wrote about it. God reminded me that we live on a planet covered with thirsty people.

Jesus knew the woman at the well needed more than a drink. She came there to draw water, yet she was thirsty for so much more. And she found something greater than what could come out of a well.[10]

In the Messiah she found love. She found the One who knew her more fully than anyone could ever know her, than she could know herself. After thirsting a long time, she finally found what she was looking for in Christ.

How often are we thirsty for Jesus, but seek drink elsewhere? How many of our friends are thirsty for the Living Water the woman at the well encountered? What will we do to make sure they take a Drink?

No, we should not become like the world. But neither should we hide from those Jesus died to save.

Not if we care.

Not if we long to fulfill His call.

Many more wait by a life's well. Let us pour out the Drink of Glory to give them life—today.

REJOICE that this ministry helps share the Invitation: This chapter first appeared in Charisma magazine. I can remember Charisma and Strang Communications partnering with Convoy of Hope to live Christ's Invitations in Orlando. Have you heard about Convoy? It provides resources to local organizations to meet physical and spiritual needs for the purpose of making communities a better place. Convoy of Hope serves in the United States and around the world providing disaster relief, building supply lines and sponsoring outreaches to the poor and hurting in communities. During a COH outreach, free groceries are distributed, job and health fairs are organized and activities for children are provided. The partnership between businesses, suppliers and Convoy of Hope has resulted in many families receiving help. www.convoyofhope.org

RELEASE your worries by praying, "God, enable me to break my rules so I can keep yours."

RECEIVE Christ's Invitation by sitting beside Jesus, confessing your sins and drinking from His Truth.

RESPOND by Inviting a friend the way Jesus would. Who will you Invite?

RENEW your mind by reading several other magazines: New Man, Spirit-Led Woman, CCM, Christianity Today, and, yes, Newsweek, Times and your local paper. Ministers should read Enrichment, Rev, IssacharFile, Leadership and Ministries Today.

Chapter 10

MISSING THE BOAT

Immediately Jesus made the disciples get into the boat and go on ahead of him to the other side, while he dismissed the crowd. After he had dismissed them, he went up on a mountainside by himself to pray. When evening came, he was there alone, but the boat was already a considerable distance from land, buffeted by the waves because the wind was against it.

During the fourth watch of the night Jesus went out to them, walking on the lake. When the disciples saw him walking on the lake, they were terrified. "It's a ghost," they said, and cried out in fear.

But Jesus immediately said to them: "Take courage! It is I. Don't be afraid."

"Lord, if it's you," Peter replied, "tell me to come to you on the water."

"Come," he said.

Then Peter got down out of the boat, walked on the water and came toward Jesus. But when he saw the wind, he was afraid and, beginning to sink, cried out, "Lord, save me!"

Immediately Jesus reached out his hand and caught him. "You of little faith," he said, "why did you doubt?"

And when they climbed into the boat, the wind died down. Then those who were in the boat worshiped him, saying, "Truly you are the Son of God."

When they had crossed over, they landed at Gennesaret. And when the men of that place recognized Jesus, they sent word to all the surrounding country. People brought all their sick to him and begged him to let the sick just touch the edge of his cloak, and all who touched him were healed.[1]

—Matthew the Disciple

If a person's peace and happiness depends on people acting as he wants them to, he will spend most of his life in unhappiness. The Gospel is not a formula whereby the believer is guaranteed that life will align with his idea of the way he believes it should be.[2]

—Malcolm Smith

Faith does not operate in the realm of the possible. There is no glory for God in that which is humanly possible. Faith begins where man's power ends.[3]

—George Muller

Many people quote that famous verse: "God helps those that help themselves." My problem? I never can locate it in Scripture.

As I read the Big Book, I realize it doesn't say that at all. It seems to say just the opposite. I journey through pages of conflict and confusion, debate and declaration, history and future, and I notice this: Those who admit their helplessness and plead for God to help are the ones getting His help. The ones who habitually help themselves, those who push forward to solve life's dilemmas with human strength and ingenuity are the ones often failing to give God an opportunity to help them. Assuming we should never confess weaknesses by calling on the Higher Power leaves us without His rescue mission. God really helps those who ask for help, declaring they can't make it without Him.

This chapter's narrative emphasizes the necessity of dependence on God. I've read it before. I've marveled at the miracle. I'm not sure I've really received the point, though. Join me as I try again.

As we plunge in, we should probably remember another common error. Once we grasp the truth of God helping those who ask for help, we open ourselves to the possibility of going to a different extreme. We might expect God to suddenly zap us, changing us into mature, flawless saints instantly. Immediate gratification orientation has trained us to believe problems can get tossed into God's spiritual microwave. We want patience. But, we want it now.

God rarely works that way. Usually, He leads us through a series of life crises—like the ones the disciples face in this story—while intending to smooth our rough edges. Rather than a quick formula or a quirky deliverance, the trials and traumas of life shape us into God's preferred people. That is His goal. That is His method. He is concerned about our comfort. But He is much more concerned about our character.

I include this story because Christ Invited Peter to come. Much different from the evangelistic Invitation of the previous chapter, this Invitation is still crucial to our view of the process of coming to Jesus. Our initial coming at conversion begins new life. It did not begin the whole journey, though. And it doesn't conclude it. Throughout the remainder of our lives we face opportunities to draw closer to our Leader. As we study this story, we should pinpoint applications in our lives. If we came to Him, we can come again.

THE CRUCIBLE OF THE DARKNESS

Five thousand men, plus women and children. That's how many they fed with five loaves of bread and two fish. How do you follow that miracle? How could Jesus match that? Once again, Jesus shocked observers with His follow-up maneuver. No press conference. No announcement of date and time and location of His next major miracle.

In what appears to be the height of missed opportunity, Jesus left. He just left. He sent away the crowd and made the disciples take a boat out on the lake. He went into the hills to pray.

What a drastic change of pace. From crowds and miracles to solitude and silence.

Then, another quick shift. The silence did not last long. Howling wind and crashing waves pierced the stillness of Christ's time alone. The disciples, having sailed about four miles, found themselves in the middle of a lake struggling against a fierce storm.[4] They faced it without the Miracle Maker in sight.

Jesus put "them forth in the danger alone, even as some mother bird thrusts her fledglings from the nest."[5] This almost appears to contradict my opening comments about helping ourselves versus depending on God. Though it appears Jesus wanted them to learn how to live without Him, let's not rush ahead too quickly. Jesus wanted His followers trusting Him. No matter the surroundings, the sounds, the storms. Isaiah asked this many years before:

> "Who among you fears the Lord and obeys the voice of his servant, who walks in darkness and has no light, yet trusts in the name of the Lord and relies upon His God?"[6]

We prefer sudden maturation. An absence of conflict would be nice. Triumph often overlooks what toiling teaches us. In the crucible of darkness we learn certain hidden truths. Too often we look for an experience of spiritual sensationalism to set us free from our immaturity. If it doesn't happen, we blame spouses or churches, and quit either or both. Church-hopping usually won't increase our character development or calm a storm. Enduring pains of life teaches us, particularly if we endure with eyes open for the Invisible One.

Why? Because of Christ's closeness. In our story, He wasn't as far from the storm riders as they assumed.

> "With the watchful eye of love, He saw them toiling in rowing...for in their Lord's absence they were able to make

no effectual progress.... It was His purpose in all the events of this night...to train his disciples to higher things than hitherto they had learned."[7]

Jesus had spent most of the night in prayer and appeared to the disciples between three and six in the morning. His means of arrival? Jesus walked on the water to them. They panicked, unable to identify the Water Walker. Was it a ghost? Into their desperation Christ spoke: "Take courage! It is I. Don't be afraid."[8]

In the classroom of a "dark and stormy night," boat riders can learn much. No matter how deep the water or how strong the storm, it helps to remember the Savior remains close. In His time He speaks. Looking for Him and listening for Him reminds riders we aren't alone.

THE COURAGE OF THE DARING

When we read the biographies of men and women who accomplished success in life, we notice a common thread. Success doesn't occur without taking risks. Living ultra-conservatively may minimize mistakes. It also impedes potential achievements. We should be wise. But, unless we occasionally venture out of the boat of safety and habit, we will never walk on the water.

In our narrative, Peter acted impulsively as usual. "Lord," he said. "If it's really You, tell me to come to You on the water." Peter the Risk-Taker assumed that if Jesus could exert enough upward force to offset gravity's attraction and remain afloat amid rapid water, He could do the same for Peter.

> "We hear a great deal about Peter's walk of faith when, taking his eye off the Lord and looking at the waves, he began to sink; but we do not hear much about the strong faith which enabled him to leave the boat, and take even a few steps on the water to Jesus."[9]

We must commend Peter's boldness. We can't fully know his motive, so we shouldn't write him off too quickly as just a loud mouth continually diving into the sea of attention. If it had been me, though, I believe my faith and courage might have been merged with a desire to prove myself. Most of my motives are a little contaminated.

Peter definitely needed more growth and development. Christ knew that. That is precisely what was about to happen.

Notice how Peter worded his statement. He did not say, "Wow, Jesus, look at You; I gotta try that." He asked Jesus to Invite him onto the water. While advocating wise risk-taking, I want to underscore this plea. An Invitation from Jesus, a Welcome, must precede such a gamble. Peter had no intention of strolling on the lake minus the Master's beckon.

Don't we often miss that? I base things on a dangerous supposition; since I'm God's child I can have what I desire and do what I want. When I act that way, God becomes merely a means to an end; that end being the satisfaction of my own greed. Our Heavenly Father wants selfishness and greed crucified, not satisfied. Infantile arrogance isn't faith. Neither is presumption.

How does it fit here, then? It is a willingness to take chances, but only as directed and protected by God. Peter asked for an Invitation. Jesus said, "Come." The word appeared so matter-of-factly, it seems Matthew reported a common event. Peter left the boat. Peter walked on the water to Jesus. He dared to leave the safety of the boat and walked toward the One calling him forth.

THE CRY OF THE DROWNING

"Peter, the experienced fisherman, who knew that the freshwater lake lacked even the partial buoyancy of the Dead Sea, left the boat. Amazed, the other disciples saw Peter walk toward Jesus. Then suddenly, Peter lost his nerve. He began to sink, and they heard a despairing cry, 'Lord, save me!'"[10]

If Peter's desire to walk on water stemmed from a hope of self-exaltation, scenes suddenly shifted that goal. Eyeing the waves and losing sight of Jesus, Peter sank. He cried for help. In front of everyone the brave Peter became the begging Peter. No time for precious words or formal prayers. He screamed, "Help!" Afraid and humbled, he expected that help. Vanity exited as water rose. Peter rapidly fidgeted, facing this fact: without Christ he could do nothing.

> "He had less real faith than he supposed, and more ardor than his faith would justify. He was rash, headlong, incautious, really attached to Jesus, but still easily daunted and prone to fall. He was afraid, therefore, when in danger, and sinking, cried again for help. Thus he was suffered to learn his own character, and his dependence on Jesus, a lesson which all Christians are permitted sooner or later to learn by dear-bought experience."[11]

I commended Peter for his willingness to take a risk. I applauded him for waiting for Christ's nod to come. Now, we might as well praise Peter's action again. As he began to sink, he certainly missed the security of the boat he departed. What did he do? He cried out to Jesus. Good move.

Why do I want to brag on that wet, afraid man? Maybe we could just say he had no other choice. Sorry to correct that view. But I know me too well. I know too many too well.

I've learned much through pastoring and counseling people who face difficult entanglements. They know Jesus. They know doctrine. Still, many stare at the waves. Many stubbornly refuse to call out to Jesus. Many refuse to do what they know to do, what they have taught others to do. They keep eyes on the water and battle with their own strength. They drown in disgusting independence.

Does that sound too simplistic? I realize many difficulties are very deep, many storms are very harsh. A casual "keep your eyes on Jesus" won't correct serious psychological dysfunctioning. On the other hand, we must not allow ourselves to overdo our therapy. The disciplines that focus our eyes on Jesus and solidify our dependency on Him are not outdated. Prayer, Bible study, worship, service and accountability cultivate our capacity to see Christ and depend on Him.

Peter didn't analyze the temperature of the water, the height of the waves or their distance from dry land. He was about to drown. So he cried for rescue.

Do we admit when we are sinking?

God wants to rescue. He can offer help when we admit we need it.

THE COMFORT OF THE DELIVER

Jesus did not delay. He reached to catch Peter. The word "caught" originated by combining words meaning "take" and "upon."[12] Jesus caught Peter and they climbed to the boat. When they were on board, the wind stopped. Jesus returned Peter to the safety of the boat and dealt with the original problem: the storm.

Notice the disciples' response. They worshipped Jesus. Their worship consisted of a confession: "Truly you are the Son of God." After the feast for five thousand, the people were satisfied. The disciples picked up the crumbs. Here, after a night of strife, they worshiped Jesus, recognizing His deity.

We love sunny days of miracles. We despise stormy nights of missing the boat. Can we, though, argue with the results? A long night ended in adoration for the Son of God.

Jesus started the evening by getting the disciples away from the crowd. Some lessons must be learned in darkness, away from noise, even religious noise. In silence Jesus reveals Himself to us in ways otherwise impossible. I usually forget that. Most of us long to mingle with multitudes, but Jesus habitually exited crowds to commune with His Father. Shouting and singing and sermonizing need to merge with silence. Richard Foster stresses the importance of this:

> "Don't you feel a tug, a yearning, to sink down into the silence and solitude of God? Don't you long for something more? Doesn't every breath crave a deeper, fuller exposure to his Presence? It is the Discipline of solitude that will open the door."[13]

Charles Swindoll tells of a poster that makes this point simply and strikingly: "My Son, slow down. Ease back. Admit your needs."[14]

When we enter the silence we can then move clearly. When we go boating at night in storming seas we can know we are not alone. When life is progressing with relative ease we will refuse the haughty lie that we are somehow capable apart from the Savior. When life slaps us hard we will refuse to tenaciously attempt to fight with our own strength. We will learn to cry "Help!" When drowning. And when sailing smoothly.

By advocating dependency on God, I'm not suggesting paralysis of incentive or creativity. Some would go too far and wait on a voice that never comes before doing what they already know to do. I am suggesting that, unless we learn that only through Christ can we accomplish ultimate good, we are faced with a terrible dilemma.

We will try, but fail, to make it on our own. The fact is, outside of Christ, we are not equipped to dive in, to survive.

The Apostle Paul understood it. Writing to a group of proud and eager Christians, he appropriately can sum up this chapter:

"I have been crucified with Christ and I no longer live, but Christ lives in me. The life I live in the body, I live by faith in the Son of God, who loved me and gave himself for me."[15]

Paul's words actually came from a stinging quote he delivered to Peter. Yes, Peter the swimmer. We learn slowly, don't we? We need constant reminding of how fruitless our efforts at helping others might be. We find ourselves on stormy seas.

When we are there, Jesus arrives. Storms and darkness don't keep Him away. Pride can. So, let's keep pride aside and call the Helper, believing He will hear and remain near. That Deliverer brings comfort even when we miss the boat.

REJOICE that this ministry helps share the Invitation: Eleos—The Care Network, Inc., is a network of innovative projects designed to strengthen the disability family. The express purpose of this organization is to embrace, elevate, and empower the disability family through faith, mentorship and community. Eleos provides opportunities of personal growth to individuals, couples and families through small group interaction, faith based counseling, church initiatives and media resources. The fundamental belief of this ministry is successful families build successful individuals. www.eleos.org

RELEASE your worries by praying, "God, my courage has wavered. Bring me back on the water with Jesus."

RECEIVE Christ's Invitation by staring at a storm and singing a song of praise to the Rescuer on His way to you.

RESPOND by Inviting a friend the way Jesus would. Who will you Invite?

RENEW your mind by writing a card to a friend. Read it again, thinking what Jesus would say if He wrote it.

Chapter 11

AWARDS, AUTOGRAPHS AND A KID IN THE MIDDLE

At that time the disciples came to Jesus and asked, "Who is the greatest in the kingdom of heaven?"

He called a little child and had him stand among them. And he said: "I tell you the truth, unless you change and become like little children, you will never enter the kingdom of heaven. Therefore, whoever humbles himself like this child is the greatest in the kingdom of heaven."[1]

—*Matthew the Tax Collector*

Here lie the beginnings of our harlotry. We cherish our lovely buildings. We give payola to pastors and missionaries so they will accept the spiritual responsibilities that releases us to acquire things. We take our wealth for granted while in our hearts the groans of the starving and the screams of the tortured are muted into the background muzak.[2]

—*John White*

> Powerlessness is a condition that frees a person to be a prophet.³
>
> —*Tony Campolo*

We now examine a very significant Invitation. Most of our narratives have given us glimpses of Christ doing the work of an evangelist or teacher. He welcomed individuals to follow Him, to travel with Him, to enter His life. In this story, He Invited a young child into the midst of His disciples, and He used the child as an illustration. The action reveals more than a gentleman's gesture of fatherly affection. It pinpoints vital truth of discipleship. Truth often overlooked by throngs around Jesus then.

Before analyzing the story, let's go back to the Garden, to the beginning. Adam, created by God and like God and for God, created to rule and subdue, was also created to commune with God as creature with Creator, friend with Friend, son with Father. The beauty of the plan tarnished when Adam listened to Eve who notified him of the serpent's suggestion to eat the fruit forbidden by God. "It won't result in death as God indicated," the snake snarled. "It will propel you to godlike status."

Eve and Adam couldn't turn down a shot at stardom. Oh, to be like God! They took the leap. Mankind has yet to stop falling. For a chance at being god, they separated themselves from God. The pull of power cost the simplicity of recognizing life's intended purpose.

As their descendents, we continue that passed-down pursuit of power. Tower of Babel. Nebuchadnezzar. Simon the Sorcerer. Crusades. Hitler. Jim Jones. September 11. Terrorist bombings. Manipulative empire builders. The endless list mirrors Adam in the garden. As humans we hear and heed the hiss of a serpent labeling God a liar: "Reach for power and it will be yours! Life is short, so go for it!" Violating the absolutes of Scripture seems innocent to us. We join masses, drunk on the desire for power.

Christ and a kid can help us.

A QUESTION

This narrative isn't an isolated occurrence. Jesus addressed the pursuit of power several times. Once, the mother of James and John lobbied for her sons to hold high positions.[4] While it is motherly and innocent to want the best for a child, the lust for power can creep in. It did for her. When our responses to our children reflect more of how their behavior affects us than them, the serpent is slithering in the grass nearby.

Similar to that Mom's request, this chapter's story begins with the disciples verbally sparring about rank in the Kingdom of Heaven. Competition. Promotion. Debate. Dispute. Such concerns, more familiar than I care to admit, reveal the hunger pains of humans craving for power. Label it selfish ambition. It is an evil longing, never ceasing its search for an answer to this question: What do I want?

When selfish ambition fuels our very existence, another step follows, almost imperceptibly. The motivation leads to serious consideration. "What do I want?," becomes, "How can I get it?" Once objectives (a nice, correct business word often used to mask greed) have been identified, the ambitious (another word more related to sin than we pretend) person like me might outline a course of action with the potential to place desire within reach. These goals (Don't you love these words?), however innocent in appearance, can turn into tiers of a personal Tower of Babel.

Did I write that too strongly? Maybe. It hits me personally; I know that. But, I must make the point. Society abounds with disastrous effects produced by seemingly harmless causes. Giving serious thought to personal agenda is dangerous. The fact that the disciples were drawn into this dialogue proves a shallowness that surely frustrated the Master.

That conversation shows the next stage in the process. Selfish ambition produced serious consideration, which eventually led to silly arguments. Peter, James and John had recently witnessed Jesus transfigured, speaking to Moses and Elijah. Not a normal day's work in my life. Then, Jesus drove a demon from an epileptic boy and restored his health, a feat the disciples attempted but failed.

Jesus sent Peter to the lake to find money for taxes in the mouth of a fish. Talk about fodder for conversation.

They could have spoken of the greatest acts ever performed on earth, but they searched for a flow chart. No wonder James later wrote how church fights come from selfish ambitions.[5] Such arguments ask the question: "Who is in my way?" Silly and sinful toxic fumes rise from the fires of selfish ambition.

A KID

As usual, Jesus taught a brief lesson in response to their question. He didn't sidestep debate to avoid self-incrimination. He used their inquiry as a springboard for discourse, and Invited a child to join them. With His live illustration in the center, Jesus told His circle of friends that they needed to change, to be "converted," to become like little children. If not, their dreams of entering the Kingdom of Heaven would never be realized. While they worried about the conditions they would find upon an arrival in Kingdom Land, Jesus spoke to them about requirements for entering.

We've probably heard about "becoming like a child." In the context of the story, Jesus only made one point. We don't need to add more meanings; Christ's lesson is challenging enough. It is also very clear: "Whoever humbles himself like this child is the greatest in the Kingdom of Heaven." The issue? Humility.

Scripture says much about humility. We are commanded to be humble and promised that, if we obey that admonition, God will lift us up.[6] Humility reigns through the Bible as a virtue leading to God's blessing. Why is such an honored attitude so absent from our daily lives? We pretend to be humble. We work to be humble. But, even our masquerade often assists us in getting our own prideful way.

Jesus used that child to underscore the weighty nature of humility. Parents may scratch their heads in wonder at His choice of an object lesson. Childishness indicates pride and selfishness, heard as the choruses of "me," "mine," and "my turn" ring out with frightening frequency. So, why pick a kid to hold up as an encouragement to be humble, as a key to enter the Kingdom?

"Jesus is not saying that children are outstanding examples of humility, or of any other virtue. He is pointing out that arrogant men and women can only possess the humility necessary for entrance into the Kingdom of heaven if they are prepared to be insignificant, as little children were in the ancient world.... A little child has no idea that he is great, and so in the Kingdom of heaven the greatest is he who is least conscious of being great."[7]

By choosing an insignificant one, Jesus made His point. Humility implies possessing no position. Benefits given by God are viewed by the humble as manifestations of grace, not favors God somehow owes His clients.

A review of church history reveals how revival movements sprang up among the nobodies of society. Laborers and common people form the nucleus of Christianity in the New Testament and in the centuries which followed. Unfortunately, revival movements often travel from humble and sincere grass roots toward cold institutionalism. Possessing powerful positions and going through religious motions minus the power of God?

Where are the humble kids when we need them?

Humility goes even farther than position issues. It demands no attention and expects no recognition. That young child did not expect Jesus to notice him. We want attention and cleverly disguise the selfish lust as doing all we can for God. Are we working for God or ourselves?

John the Baptist determined to decrease so Christ could increase.[8] We think that if we can only increase, Christ will increase as well. The Apostle Paul learned through tribulation and unanswered prayer that at our weakest point we are strongest.[9]

Maybe as nobodies, God can actually do through us what He longs to do. The New Testament analogy of the Body of Christ beautifully emphasizes how operational the church can be when made up of parts working together for the good of the whole. If we could grasp the awesome truth of our significance to Christ, we would be less likely to attempt proving our worth by becoming "somebodies" in the eyes of others.

For those who have faithfully labored in the field of God's service, please do not get tired of anonymity. Lack of recognition may be a greater blessing than you know. Don't seek the attention of men. Be obedient to your True Lover. Remain humble. Better to walk low and let God do the exalting that to walk tall and receive God's correction.

Dear child, go after God's attention. That is what matters.

A KINGDOM

Do those thoughts appear harsh? They do to me. I often fail to remember how Christ's Kingdom drastically differs from our world system. Jesus abolished the pecking order. There is no top rung. God is the only CEO of Kingdom Life; His servants merely toil where He plants us to use the grace gifts He places within us. True glory can only go to God. How does it do that? Notice three ways the Kingdom reverses trends of humans hungry for power.

Gaining By Giving

An understanding of the principle of gaining more by giving away would drastically alter our present approaches. This isn't carnal calls to "give me money so God can heal you." This is letting go of what we want, what we think we somehow deserve, what we feel owed. Giving, in that real, crucifying sense, must emerge as a driving force in our behavior. Not only would this smack a severe blow to religious materialism, but it might allow us to return to the freedom and simplicity of grasping less while gaining more. Much more.

Leading By Serving

Jesus led His followers with strength, not weakness. But the prime evidence of Christ's strength was His humility.[10] His cloak of leadership wasn't a shining robe. It was a towel. He wrapped Himself with it to wash His followers' feet.[11] Because we sometimes succumb to, or participate in, the religious manipulation of our day, we should read the words of that Foot Washer:

"The kings of the Gentiles lord it over them; and those who exercise authority over them call themselves Benefactors. But you are not like that. Instead, the greatest among you should be like the youngest, and the one who rules like the one who serves. For who is greater, the one who is at the table or the one who serves? Is it not the one who is at the table? But I am among you as one who serves."[12]

With His life and words Jesus presided over the funeral for all forms of authoritarianism and manipulation in His Kingdom. Leader equals servant.

Winning By Losing

No one likes to lose, especially me. I am a typical male with a strong desire to succeed and conquer. I can't relax on vacations until I have arrived safely back home—on time, within budget, all plans accomplished while there—thus, winning the contest. Despite such common and inherent drives, competition can corrupt us. In the Kingdom, we win Life by losing our idea of how we think life should work.[13] We live by dying to self. A frightening pastime of religious competition might keep us moving rapidly while speeding far from our Father.

First place isn't synonymous with His place.

Jesus told a parable that compared the Kingdom to a seed that became a large plant housing birds in its branches.[14] Today's trends lure us toward devising schemes for the "kingdom plant." We try to fence it in. We charge admission to outsiders wanting to see our plant. We stand beside, smiling as pictures are taken. We make replicas and award models to those who sing the best songs or write the best stories about the "plant." We make money while God grows nauseous. We are oblivious to the fact that the plant is slowly dying.

Awards.

Autographs.

Or a kid in the middle.

His Invitation is to be like the child.

REJOICE that this ministry helps share the Invitation: Church planting has become a major thrust of the International Pentecostal

Holiness Church. Through their REACH 3, PLANT 3 emphasis, they are asking each member to reach three people for Christ. Each church is challenged to plant three daughter congregations: one like itself, one cross-culturally, and one beyond national borders. Sounds like what Jesus would do, doesn't it?

www.iphc.org

RELEASE your worries by praying, "God, I'm sorry for trying to make myself important."

RECEIVE Christ's Invitation by hearing a Voice call you into His arms.

RESPOND by Inviting a friend the way Jesus would. Who will you Invite?

RENEW your mind by writing this passage with your name included. Use it as a journal to find out where you are and where you need to be. Remember: you are Invited!

Chapter 12

LEAVING THE BACK DOOR OPEN

Now a man came up to Jesus and asked, "Teacher, what good thing must I do to get eternal life?"

"Why do you ask me about what is good?" Jesus replied. "There is only One who is good. If you want to enter life, obey the commandments."

"Which ones?" the man inquired.

Jesus replied, "'Do not murder, do not commit adultery, do not steal, do not give false testimony, honor your father and mother,' and 'love your neighbor as yourself.'"

"All these I have kept," the young man said. "What do I still lack?"

Jesus answered, "If you want to be perfect, go, sell your possessions and give to the poor, and you will have treasure in heaven. Then come, follow me."

When the young man heard this, he went away sad, because he had great wealth.

Then Jesus said to his disciples, "I tell you the truth, it is hard for a rich man to enter the kingdom of heaven. Again I tell you, it is easier for a camel to go through the eye of a needle than for a rich man to enter the kingdom of God."

> When the disciples heard this, they were greatly astonished and asked, "Who then can be saved?"
>
> Jesus looked at them and said, "With man this is impossible, but with God all things are possible."
>
> Peter answered him, "We have left everything to follow you! What then will there be for us?"
>
> Jesus said to them, "I tell you the truth, at the renewal of all things, when the Son of Man sits on his glorious throne, you who have followed me will also sit on twelve thrones, judging the twelve tribes of Israel. And everyone who has left houses or brothers or sisters or father or mother or children or fields for my sake will receive a hundred times as much and will inherit eternal life. But many who are first will be last, and many who are last will be first."[1]
> —*Matthew*

> It is always more difficult to sing when the audience has turned its back.[2]
> —*Calvin Miller*

> Divorce me, unite, or break that knot again.
> Take me to You, imprison me, for I
> Except You enthrall me, never shall be free;
> Nor ever chaste, except You ravish me.[3]
> —*John Donne*

Church growth. That theme lures me. I preach on Sundays and stare at the people I love. I only wish many more would join us. Missions and ministries, local outreach and global dreams, large churches and small churches: I want more people to join our ranks.

I'm not alone. Books and seminars and committees and corpora-

Leaving the Back Door Open

tions and trends and sites about church growth abound. One of the most popular themes tells guys like me how to "close the back door." That theme refers to ways local churches can prevent those attending from leaving to find other church homes or depart churches completely.

Attracting newcomers is important. But, to grow numerically and teach those we reach, we must keep those who have arrived. Most congregations would hit astounding numbers if all those who attended the building in the last year became regular members.

As I type these words, I feel a strange range of feelings. Today is Thursday. Each of the previous days this week, I heard from people about why they left a local church. I hurt. I care. I struggle finishing what is my last chapter to finally complete. I've been asking God a lot of questions.

One of my friends has been a Christian for many years. He has been a key leader in several churches. Now? He blames churches for his battles and attends no church at all. I pray he finds a home and enters there with courage. Not a perfect local church, since none exist. Just a family that will welcome him and give him time to heal.

One family left our local church without telling me. The last news I received was that my sermons changed their lives, our family welcomed them with kindness, and God answered all their prayers by bringing them to us. I believed them. A ministry friend told me not to get my hopes up. Too late. They were up, way up. After not seeing this family, I called them. They apologized as they told me they had left and now attend another church. I prayed God would bless them before hanging up the phone. Then, I cried, asking God what I did wrong.

The other friend just returned from a long time involved in a small church. They hardly let her go. They accused, abused and confused her precious heart for ministry. Now, we pray God gives her peace. Maybe she will stay with us. But, wherever she goes, she must never enter a cave of control again.

So, see how I feel?

As I hurt for those three true stories, I type letters on a keyboard, remembering an ancient story.

I hope we reach people and retain them. But, I pray we never become preoccupied with visible success. Names and numbers aren't enough. In the spirit realm, success is difficult to measure. You deal in terms of community building and character development—factors that often elude simple measurement. To satisfy our needs to gauge success, then, we turn to the external signs. They are visible and measurable. We count members and money and register the totals. High numbers equal success; low numbers indicate failure.

Then we read these ancient stories of Jesus the Inviter.

> An old Bob Bennett song comes to my mind,
> "You can show me your sales curves
> Plot my life on a flow chart
> But there's just some things
> That numbers can't measure
> In Matters of the Heart."[4]

We believe in the importance of evangelism. Winning people for God is not an option for His people. Every Christian and every church body should put forth effort to fulfill the Great Commission. Somehow, though, priorities might change in normal people like us. We might move from winning the lost to winning the contest. The shift is subtle. A sincere desire to reach the world for Christ weds itself to a carnal desire to possess the most powerful enterprise.

The proliferation of marketing schemes and magnetic dreams promise that if we operate the way other successful leaders have operated, victories will parallel theirs. Unfortunately, many well-meaning leaders implement hand-me-down programs on the advice of the experts and, in the end, frustrate themselves and accomplish very little.

Jesus did not have the advantage of attending a church growth seminar. Or, the disadvantage. He did not even seem to understand the method of "closing the back door." His stat sheet points to a willingness to leave the back door open.

He gladly let people come to Him. He also let them leave.

He opened a door of welcome to all who expressed interest. He also, though sadly, let deserters go when they chose to go.

He never altered His message to gain a convert. The story called The Rich Young Ruler uncovers the technique of Jesus leaving the back door open.

LET THEM COME

Christ was not impressed by status, education, ability or heritage. He saw people as needy, regardless of how effectively they disguised their neediness. His list of candidates to welcome? The poor and rich, the young and old. The males and females, the religious and pagan. He let them come. He let them all come.

Prior to the scenario of The Rich Ruler, Jesus proved His indiscriminate policy. By placing His hands on a group of youngsters the disciples had told to scram, Jesus informed His followers that the entrenched caste system no longer applied. Children, given no place by the establishment, were welcomed. Women, viewed as mere servants, could also come. The poor, considered cursed monetarily because of moral flaws, were given lower spiritual status. But Jesus let them come unto Him. All of them.

In this story, a wealthy young ruler came to Jesus. He came running. He then screeched to a halt by kneeling at the feet of the One he called, "Good Teacher." At the man's inquiry, Jesus did not judge or reject Him. He didn't label the man without listening to Him. Good policy and great practice. Why? Jesus' method was to receive people—all people. Though many rejected Him, He did not reject them.

Do we really allow all people to come? Or does our religious machinery grind people up and spit them out before they ever experience Christ? We impress with our luxurious buildings. We hypnotize with our oratory. We instruct them to tithe; we inspire them to teach. I often wonder if those who come near me really see Jesus or if they merely notice evidence of my efforts at ingenuity.

Many are so turned off by elaborate approaches that they never darken doors of our multi-million dollar religious convention centers. Rich young rulers would feel more comfortable in these modern Meccas of merchandising than would a woman at the well. Or a

Simon Peter. Or a John the Baptist. Or maybe even a carpenter from Nazareth. Jesus never compromised His message, but He was easily accessible.

But, more of that later. For now, let's realize Jesus let that man come to Him. Jesus had time for him.

LET THEM KNOW

Jesus was a disastrous politician. When opportunities arose that could boost His popularity, He opened His mouth and breathed fire. He wasn't cruel, He just had a major problem: He always spoke the Truth.

No bending of facts. No tickling of ears. No showing only the good side for the camera. No laugh tracks to prime the pumps of participants. He called it like He saw it, like He knew it, like it was. This presented constant problems because Jesus saw life from the spiritual/eternal perspective while those around Him watched life wearing material/temporal glasses.

Jesus responded to the rich man's address: "Why do you call me good? No one deserves that title but God alone." That statement took another look at the rich man's greeting of courtesy. Jesus made a mockery of the religious cliché.

The man had rushed to Jesus unaware of the Person he knelt beside. Christ did not deflect the term "good" because He lacked the virtue of goodness. He underscored the exclusivity of that title stressing that only God should be addressed that way.

What was Jesus saying? The man wanted helpful advice from a teacher. In the process, he stumbled upon God. Jesus did not reject the label, but the ruler's faulty understanding of Deity.

Notice the dialogue.

Jesus: "Obey the commands."
Rich Man: "I have."
Jesus: "Well, to be complete, do one more thing. Sell your possessions to provide for the poor."

To a culture viewing wealth as a sign of God's blessing, Jesus pointed a seeker to the road of poverty. Or, maybe to the road to recovery.

Jesus Invited the Rich Man to follow Him. But the wealthy questioner never made it that far. The cost was too high. The Truth too painful.

Christianity's good news equals bad news to our self-sufficiency. Wealth, viewed as a blessing, seemed to be described by Jesus as a potential hindrance. Jesus wanted Him to readjust a good thing in order to allow himself time with a Much Greater Thing. Jesus wanted the man to get his distraction out of the way.

Jesus stated "a law of life when he said that where one's treasure is, there the heart will be also. He would clearly have liked to enroll the rich man among his disciples, and up to a point the rich man was not unwilling to become one of them. But the sticking point came when he was asked to unburden himself of his property."[5]

Jesus pointed out the obstacle in the listener's life. After letting the man come to Him, Jesus clearly told that man the truth. As it often is, the Truth then was painful.

LET THEM GO

Letting people come and letting people know both fall under the category of evangelism. But letting people go? That doesn't seem to fit.

Jesus let people see Him, visit Him. He pushed no one away and He never wavered in presenting the Truth. When an inquirer refused His message, Jesus would let that person go.

Don't you struggle with this? I do. Where was Christ's follow-up call? That man had major potential. How could Jesus keep Matthew and let this questioning seeker get away? My Bible doesn't include this quote in any of Christ's conversations with another person. So, why there? Why then? Why him? I have shelves of church growth books Jesus needed at that moment.

Of course, we must not let people leave church families without calling them or Inviting them back. That would be insensitive. Nor should we take a casual, uncaring approach when people reject Jesus. That would be cruel.

But, this narrative does balance this book's theme. In Mark's version we read that Jesus loved the young man. The rich ruler wasn't the only one saddened by the decision; Jesus felt it. Christ's true love, though, is precisely what kept Him from softening the message and pleading with him to stay.

Notice the balance through the Bible. A Shepherd left 99 sheep just to find a lost one.[6] No expense should be spared to claim back the stray. Yet, Jesus did not seek to turn Christianity into a cult of Keeping Followers Under Control.

A father allowed a son to leave home. He did not chase him. He did not search for him. When the son returned, Dad embraced him and granted him back to family status.

What can we learn? Let's learn to care while refusing to babysit. As a pastor, I wonder how many times my Chris care has stood in the way of Christ's care. I'm sure I've interfered with God's one-on-one dealings with others because I hated to see them ride away.

Becky Pippert wrote, "Nurture and love is one thing, playing God in someone's life is another."[7] To pastors, to parents, to all people who care, the message is this: When people walk out we have no choice but to let them go.

A ministry friend told me 24 out of every 25 students entering the ministry quit within 25 years. Why? Many factors contribute, but a main cause is the inability to let people go.

Does this go even farther? What if they fall? Paul suggested three times that unrepentant sinners should be turned over to Satan.[8] God's loving discipline is not enough. Some people become so calloused to the Spirit that only a trip into a destructive demonic trap can sink them low enough to wake them from the destruction.

I once heard Bob Mumford tell of a time when, as a six-year-old, he disobeyed his mother. She was distraught and gave him a choice as to the punishment. She would either spank him or not speak to him. He chose the silent treatment. After only an hour he begged for the spanking. When we let people go, God's silent treatment works them over in ways our badgering or begging never could.[9]

Jesus let people know the Truth. That Truth cost disciples and followers. Ultimately, it cost Him His life. But, to the grave and back, Jesus never stopped telling the Truth.

To people depending on their wealth or their works, Jesus made it clear that all human efforts fall far short of God.

To those worshiping the wrong things, Jesus proclaimed that nothing lasts apart from God.

To all, Jesus shouted that the bargaining chips will run out before the jackpot comes.[10]

He let people come. He wasn't interested in who, where or what they had been.

He let people know the Truth and was not intimidated by them.

If they received the Word, He gladly received them. If they rejected the Word, He sadly let them go.

He does the same with us. We must do the same with others.

REJOICE that this ministry helps share the Invitation: I love teamwork among different groups and denominations. As a part of the Assemblies of God, I appreciate our goal to apply Christ's Invitations. Our purpose is to be an agency of God for evangelizing the world, to be a corporate body in which people may worship God and to be a channel of God's purpose to build a body of saints being perfected in the image of His Son. www.ag.org

RELEASE your worries by praying, "God, help me get rid of anything standing between us."

RECEIVE Christ's Invitation by refusing to walk away from Jesus.

RESPOND by Inviting a friend the way Jesus would. Who will you Invite?

RENEW your mind by reading books by George Barna, George Wood, Lee Grady, Leonard Sweet, Sergio Scataglini and Chuck Swindoll.

Chapter 13

NO SUDDEN MOVES, PLEASE

Large crowds were traveling with Jesus, and turning to them he said: "If anyone comes to me and does not hate his father and mother, his wife and children, his brothers and sisters—yes, even his own life—he cannot be my disciple. And anyone who does not carry his cross and follow me cannot be my disciple.

"Suppose one of you wants to build a tower. Will he not first sit down and estimate the cost to see if he has enough money to complete it? For if he lays the foundation and is not able to finish it, everyone who sees it will ridicule him, saying, 'This fellow began to build and was not able to finish.'

"Or suppose a king is about to go to war against another king. Will he not first sit down and consider whether he is able with ten thousand men to oppose the one coming against him with twenty thousand? If he is not able, he will send a delegation while the other is still a long way off and will ask for terms of peace. In the same way, any of you who does not give up everything he has cannot be my disciple.

"Salt is good, but if it loses its saltiness, how can it be made salty again? It is fit neither for the soil nor for the manure pile; it is thrown out.

"He who has ears to hear, let him hear."[1]

—*Luke the Physician*

And he calls us to follow him, to follow him, that is, in his amazing capacity to ignore the demands of his bodily and emotional needs and be concerned with others. The pathway is uninviting, impossibly steep, but rewarding. We cannot climb it without divine aid.[2]

—*John White*

We explain clearly and honestly the cost of discipleship and let each person decide whether or not to pay it. If he decides he can't, we weep. If he decides he can, we don't give him a prize or pat him on the back. We start paying the cost together.[3]

—*Mike Yaconelli*

Vegetables and I never had a close relationship during my childhood. My friends farmed them, my family cleaned them, my mother cooked them and everybody but me ate them. My parents attempted to persuade me to eat them, playing my role in promoting a heritage and remaining healthy as I did.

Their tricks and tests didn't work. Parental experts, family counselors and practical therapists might instruct those in authority to never let their picky-little-Chris eat anything until he ate those ugly, stinky, green goodies. They tried. I almost died. I chose starvation instead of tasting, swallowing, digesting the veggies that would bring health to my skinny bones.

Now? I'm still a cautious eater. Others would choose other words to use but I typed cautious. I eat vegetables now, though rarely. Preferring them plain instead of cooked and flavored, I slowly learned not to waste health because of preferred taste. Healthy diets include all the needed foods, not just those flavors my selfishness would favor.

So goes the gospel. Jesus didn't limit His strategy to what taste buds ordered. He cooked and served meals of truth. His fruits and vegetables challenged the hungry to make decisions. Some swallowed what He served. Some avoided His fresh feasts. Today His ancient menu remains true. And available. And challenging. Will we accept it? Will we avoid it? Or will we grab it, stir it and remake it into what we think today's eaters prefer?

To find out, let us visit Him and question ourselves. As Jesus walked, thronged by an impressed crowd of seekers, He held no gun to the head of potential disciples. He did tell them about life hanging on an edge, about keeping balance, about making sudden moves. A large crowd ready to order, longing to eat whatever He served, Jesus refused to market His ministry by playing into their emotions. He didn't jerk their tears with a story or wrench their guts with a solo. He didn't pressure or push. He didn't play into the get-a-crowd-and-keep-it-growing game.

Instead, Jesus warned potential followers about the pitfalls of moving suddenly to follow Him. He shattered their romantic ideals, punctured their political agendas and cautioned any impulsive jumps onto the bandwagon. Honestly I think He acted exactly the opposite of how I think He should have. But that's why I'm here and He was there. His voice almost carried a sign: "Danger Ahead...Proceed With Caution."

HATE

If Jesus came to speak in English, a language, let's say, that He doesn't know, and picked me as the interpreter, how would I react to this statement? I would not want my friends or my sons to hear Him talk about hating parents. Glancing toward Jesus my body language and facial expressions might show Him my shock, disapproval and desire to interpret the comments much differently.

Jesus, saying a person disqualifies himself from discipleship unless he hates his family members and his own life, opened the door of excuses for parent-haters, self-haters, and depressed, downtrodden, desperate, defeated addicts. What about the meaning of the word; would that help us? "Hate" meant then and there what it means here and now: to abhor, to detest.

Though the statement appears to run counter to demands dictated by responsibility, decency and to what the whole Christian life represents, Jesus chose such a harsh four-letter word to illustrate vital truth. He alerted listeners. He shocked seekers. He warned wonderers. But why that way?

F. F. Bruce offers an answer:

> "What does it mean then? It means that, just as property can come between us and the kingdom of God, so can family ties. The interests of God's kingdom must be paramount with the followers of Jesus, and everything else must take second place to them, even family ties....[A] man or woman might be so bound up by family ties as to have no time or interest for matters of greater moment than the kingdom of God....If 'hating' one's relatives is felt to be a shocking idea, it was meant to be shocking, to shock the hearers into a sense of the imperious demands of the Kingdom of God. We know that a biblical idiom to hate can mean to love less."[4]

Paul drew a similar contrast between Kingdom life and worldly life. He stated that he had lost all things for Christ, adding the commentary that he considered items lost as only rubbish.[5] Such thoughts must not be isolated and used as proof texts for irresponsibility or family neglect. Christ's dialogue merges with the whole of Scripture. Too many well-meaning but driven Christian leaders sacrifice families on the altar of religious achievement. They work any hours, break any promise, make any excuse if the ministry is at stake. Jesus espoused no such heresy.

The Jesus who taught us to love enemies most certainly wants us to love family and friends. But our love for them, and our love for ourselves, appears as hate when placed beside unwavering, uncommon, uncompromising love for our Heavenly Father. If Father says pray, attend church, preach or travel to a foreign land, family pressures should not hinder as long as family commitments and obligations do not go lacking. Otherwise we can't be His disciples.

DIE

Does it get easier? No. In verse 27 we hear Jesus focus on our next word: die. We frequently elaborate on the glories of the abundant life promised us by Christ. Just as frequently we ignore the promise of daily death. "Take up the cross" means far more than donning a shining crucifix as a necklace. It also speaks of much more than bearing the cross of the regular burden-load that continually climbs on our backs. Jesus said to follow Him one must die; that is the portion painted by the word "cross."

Again, we can learn from Bruce:

> "The sight of a man being taken to the place of public crucifixion was not unfamiliar in the Roman world of that day. Such a man was commonly made to carry the crossbeam, the patibulum, of his cross as he went to his death. That is the picture which Jesus' words would conjure up in the minds of hearers. If they were not prepared for that outcome to their discipleship, let them change their minds while there was time—but first let them weight the options in the balances of the Kingdom of God...."[6]

Today, Christ might say to a modern audience, "Take your place on death row and follow me. Follow me if you choose, just remember you will be living only a short walk away from the electric chair." We like to think that when we align ourselves with Jesus we assume a place in a line of humanity that is guaranteed to receive the handouts of monetary gain, marital bliss, ministry success and a multitude of friends. Jesus' words remind us otherwise. While righteousness, peace and joy await us, we are lining up for the gas chamber when we say yes to His invitation. Maybe we should alter the words of the musical refrain and sing with commitment: "Come and die, the Master calleth, come and die."

Paul confessed to dying daily. He said, "Those who belong to Christ have crucified the sinful nature with its passions and desires."[7] Are we exempt to a rule Jesus laid down? Though persecution and crucifixion are foreign to many believers, voices of faithful martyrs around the world and across time force us to acknowledge this: Believing means more than a little ridicule or rejection. It means blood. His. And ours. Unless we face that we cannot be His disciples.

COUNT

Jesus then told two stories, giving us our third verb: count. That word falls in the middle of our list, serving as the main thrust of the narrative. Do not follow Christ without counting the cost.

A building contractor wouldn't begin construction without reconciling an estimate of expected expenditures with money available and profits to be earned. He counts the cost. A president wouldn't declare war on a nation that his troops stood no chance against. He calls together advisers, weighs alternatives, predicts results, observes optional strategies and political ramifications. He counts the cost.

We live in an era of instant decisions and immediate returns. Toss a plate of food into the microwave and cook a meal in minutes. Board a plane and crisscross the country in hours. Order a burger with fries and start eating while receiving drive-through change. Credit cards have eliminated the need to save before making a purchase. We work later for what the plastic provides now. Careful consideration rarely enters the equation of our decision making process.

It was to a much different type of world that Jesus said, "Count the cost." But two thousand years later He continues to voice the caution. When souls lean toward hell should we encourage them to look, really look for a while, before they leap into Christianity? Does God want us to be shorter on emotional appeals and longer on factual presentations? I don't want to. My statistics might slow, my friends might stay lost, my audience might choose to refuse to follow Jesus.

Following Christ is a reality individuals experience subjectively, but the Bible reveals that the decision to enter that encounter is to be weighed objectively. Christ knocks at the door. He doesn't pick the lock.[8] He doesn't break in. Before a person opens the door Jesus wants them to know the danger of His entrance.

DENY

Verse 33 presents another verb: deny. In our lust for pleasure and comfort we often forget the road of self-denial. We usually opt to travel Self-gratification Street or Self-indulgent Drive. Jesus said, "Give it up." His word meant to place away from, to say farewell to, to renounce, to take a leave of. Listeners could relate since many of them standing nearby had literally given all to follow Him.[9]

Why do many in today's world come to Christ? Often they dive in after hearing an appeal about how He would give them anything they want, that He would make them feel good.[10] Where do such theories come from? If Christianity is only a sound investment promising amazing temporal returns on a few minor inconveniences, why would anyone stay away? Believe in Jesus and inherit a new, top-of-the-line automobile! I think we know Who isn't laughing.

The Holy Truth is more than a game show. Pity those who reduce it to one.

Paul said, "Nobody should seek his own good, but the good of others."[11] The ugly truth is that most of us are so concerned with our own needs we become blind to the needs of others nearby or around the world. The god of self has ascended the throne and sits in a seat reserved for King Jesus. Our flesh welcomes the robbery.

Becky Pippert sums it up:

> "Whenever our life is in conflict with God's truth as revealed in the Bible, we must change. When the self contradicts the will of God, we deny the self. When the self chooses sin, we say no to it. When the self wants to put our interest above the interest of others, we side with love against the self....To live the way of the cross means to say yes to God and no to self." [12]

Does this point to self-flagellation or monastic living? No. Once again we must understand the thought in light of the whole of Scripture. A person must be willing to give up all to follow Christ. Without such a radical commitment to selfless living we can't be His disciples.

ENDURE

Jesus' comments about salt point to one more verb: endure. The salt that preserves, heals, makes thirsty and adds flavor is not good once it loses that which makes it salt. It isn't good for flavoring food. Neither for the manure pile. He who endures to the end, and thus stays salty, will be saved. He who doesn't will be thrown out. The original audience knew that "salt was rarely found in a pure state; in practice it was mixed with other substances, various forms of earth. So long as the portion of salt in the mixture was sufficiently high, the mixture would serve the purpose of true salt. But if, through exposure to damp or some other reason, all the salt mixture was leeched out, what was left was good for nothing."[13]

Has salt mixture been leeched out of our lives? Have we failed to endure to the end as an influence in the world? Though we started out shining, have we grown dim?

Just as most of us pursue the instant gratification of self at a frantic pace, we seem equally intent on giving up if our expectations aren't quickly met. We live in a society of quitters. When candles of romance burn out we quit marriages rather than working to restore the flame. When the barbs of differences surface, we quit relationships rather than learning lessons of acceptance and forgiveness. When excitement of newness turns into routine we quit church involvement rather than doing our part to help the wind blow again. When expected changes elude us we quit our Bible reading and prayer rather than keeping devotional commitments as a way of life.

Such a mindset of giving up leaves us without saltiness. We fail to endure. As salt we are the hope of a better world. When we lose our capacity to improve life, we also lose our capacity to find true Life ourselves. To be His disciple is to maintain the salt mixture.

Crowds followed Jesus but only a few committed disciples started the wheels rolling for a radical world change. Crowds impress but disciples change a world. Crowds tally up nicely for show but disciples tenaciously resist the mixture of evil. Crowds heard those ancient words of Jesus; the few who heeded the statements became disciples.

No Sudden Moves, Please

Where do you fit? Are you part of the multitude of Christ's acquaintances, those who know about Him and follow Him in pursuit of comfort and happiness? Or are you one of the disciples? If you are a disciple, you know about these verbs and their important interplay in everyday life. Jesus made clear the line that must be crossed. Don't be content as a mere face in the crowd of professing ones. Cross the line. Line up at the cross. If we do we may lose life or limb. At the least we will see self topple from the throne. We will also be instrumental in changing the world for Jesus and being changed ourselves in His image.

Count the cost. Weigh the options carefully. We live with our decision. Forever.

REJOICE that this ministry helps share the Invitation: Charlie's Lunch began in 1997, when Sam and Janey Stewart returned to Guatemala to continue their missionary work after their second son, Charlie, had suddenly passed away on the mission field. Charlie was known for his giving and loving heart. (He would accompany his dad in his missionary work and always come home with empty pockets because he had given away everything he had.) At each feeding, Bible stories, verses, songs and personal hygiene are taught. The children are taught how important they are and how much God loves them. Today, Charlie's Lunch has feeding centers in Guatemala, El Salvador, Mexico and India, feeding over 800 children regularly. www.charlieslunch.org

RELEASE your worries by praying, "God, strengthen my commitment today. Help me endure to the end."

RECEIVE Christ's Invitation by making a list of things you love too much and ways you give up too quickly.

RESPOND by Inviting a friend the way Jesus would. Who will you Invite?

RENEW your mind by reading books by Rebecca Pippert, John Eldridge, Christopher DeVinck and Jamie Buckingham.

Chapter 14

BEGGARS CAN BE CHOSEN

Then they came to Jericho. As Jesus and his disciples, together with a large crowd, were leaving the city, a blind man, Bartimaeus (that is, the Son of Timaeus), was sitting by the roadside begging. When he heard that it was Jesus of Nazareth, he began to shout, "Jesus, Son of David, have mercy on me!"

Many rebuked him and told him to be quiet, but he shouted all the more, "Son of David, have mercy on me!"

Jesus stopped and said, "Call him."

So they called to the blind man, "Cheer up! On your feet! He's calling you." Throwing his cloak aside, he jumped to his feet and came to Jesus.

"What do you want me to do for you?" Jesus asked him.

The blind man said, "Rabbi, I want to see."

"Go," said Jesus, "your faith has healed you." Immediately he received his sight and followed Jesus along the road.[1]

—Mark

> Our friendship with God should be so clear that we can depend on Him not to turn us away, therefore continuing to pray until He answers.[2]
> —*Andrew Murray*

> There's a table ready and waiting
> There's a place that is set just for you
> You can feast for a lifetime of living
> It can happen if you want it to
> If you want it to
> Well, I'm a Beggar
> But I know where there's bread
> I'm a Beggar
> But now I'm so well fed
> If you're hungry why will you suffer instead
> Come along.[3]
> —*Bob Bennett*

Beggars, the saying says, can't be choosy. By depending on the assistance of others they disqualify themselves from pickiness. Too much scrutiny can drive away needed help. The phrase means that if you are going to beg, take what's given to you.

Observing Christ's march into Jericho, let's twist the saying. Jesus did. In the process, He taught a lesson that should make us leap for joy. Or kneel in awe. Beggars might not be permitted to be choosy, but this encounter teaches us that beggars can be chosen. In the real world of corporations and competition where firm handshakes and shapely figures propel workaholics to high places, few beggars get picked. People work for it, study for it, strive for it. Some are born into it. Some are simply called lucky. Beggars, who strip away their pride and uninhibitedly reveal their helplessness, get little chance to arrive. They usually get left out in the choosing.

Jesus bucked that trend. He welcomed beggars instead of pushing them aside. He showed an affinity for the unprotected who admitted their nakedness and asked to be clothed. He helped those who neither tried to cover their nakedness themselves nor enjoyed their humiliating condition, but chose to voice their hopes for help. Beggars: unpopular then and unpopular now. But, then and now, when begging occurs properly, a Helper might visit those seeking help.

THE CRY

Jesus had just finished lecturing the disciples about the dangers of pride. Then He walked into a crowd. Voices raised volume. People pushed for a chance to see that Man whose reputation preceded Him. They glanced, stared, listened and walked in His direction. Suddenly a cry could be heard above the clamor. The voice? A beggar. The purpose? He hoped that Popular Leader would hear him. His plea? A shout for mercy.

Pride didn't cloak his insecurities or deny his true conditions. Bartimaeus, the blind beggar, had no one to impress. Pleading in desperation, he cried for a cure. Tension from years of humiliation rode through his petition. He refused to clothe his nervousness with courtesy. He screamed dreams of departing his common curse. Maybe he told himself his day had come. Maybe that would be his final chance to find change.

How often do hurting hearts incorrectly assume that, since God knows everything anyway, time shouldn't be wasted by praying and pleading? Sincerely not wishing to order God—as some seem to enjoy attempts of—the errors hit an opposite end. No crying to God. Struggling with hopes, solving problems, concluding that God helps when and if He sees fit, begging has no place.

Refusing to treat Almighty God as a cosmic bellhop is a good thing. But failing to pray is wrong. It damages God's people. It disappoints God. It disobeys His commands. It distances the needy from His Hands. Like Bartimaeus, we do not fully see. We lack much. We are beggars. Unlike Bartimaeus, we refuse to cry frantically for God to rescue us.

Prayer permits us to admit our helplessness. It allows us to participate in the movement of God. What a privilege! Allowed to join God in seeing His work accomplished? An honor! The omnipotent (all-powerful) and omniscient (all-knowing) Creator often waits for our cry before taking action.

Crowds of beggars walked past Jesus. Many chose to remain where they were, as they were, refusing to howl for help. Bartimaeus cried until Jesus could hear him.

Andrew Murray wrote,

> "What a deep heavenly mystery prevailing prayer is! The God Who has promised and Who longs to give the blessing holds it back. It is a matter of such deep importance to Him that His friends on earth should know and fully trust their Friend in heaven! Because of this, He trains them in the school of delayed answer to find out how their perseverance really does prevail. They can wield mighty power in heaven if they simply set themselves to it."[4]

THE CRITICISM

His friends, family, the denominational committee and the neighborhood watch commission voted to veto his screams. Their schemes would not allow such a distraction. That makes sense, doesn't it? Bartimaeus lacked courtesy. Jesus, busy and in constant demand, stood in the middle of a large audience. He needed to leave that city and be about His Father's business. An interruption by a neighborhood street bum's screams fell under the heading of unnecessary demands on the already overworked Messiah.

People pour cold water into faith these days, also. They feel it is okay if we serve God as long as we do not go overboard. We don't need to take this Christianity stuff too seriously. Parents often pray rebellious teens into salvation. Then, when the conversion comes, it might include excitement, zeal and evidence of a radical commitment, qualities that lead parents to accusing those spiritual babies of going overboard.

When critics turn fire extinguishers on the flames of faith, Bartimaeuses should keep believing. When told to silence their faith, Bartimaeuses must shout even more. Bartimaeus did then. He cried on, concerned with catching the attention of Christ and unaffected by the critics.

The more acute the condition the less the crying one cares what others think. Bartimaeus continued crying out. His vision overlooked the critics. His hopes rested in Christ alone.

Frederick Buechner applauds such tenacity:

> "According to Jesus, by far the most important thing about praying is to keep at it. The images he uses to explain this are all rather comic, as though he thought it was rather comic to have to explain it at all. He says God is like a friend you go to borrow bread from at midnight. The friend tells you in effect to drop dead, but you go on knocking anyway until finally he gives you what you want so he can go back to bed again (Luke 11:5-8). Or God is like a crooked judge who refuses to hear the case of a certain poor widow, presumably because he knows there's nothing much in it for him. But she keeps on hounding him until finally he hears her case just to get her out of his hair (Luke 18:1-8). Even a stinker, Jesus says, won't give his own son a black eye when he asks for peanut butter and jelly, so how all the more will God when his children (Matthew 7:9-11). Be importunate, Jesus says—not one assumes because you have to beat a path to God's door before he'll open it, but because until you beat the path maybe there's no way of getting to your door."[5]

THE CALL

Then came two words Bartimaeus hoped to hear. Jesus stopped. He turned toward those keeping a block between the shouter and the Listener. He voiced His Invitation, "Call him."

How wonderful those two words must have sounded to a beggar accustomed to rejection. An Invitation! A welcome from the

Messiah! Jesus, son of David, said, "Call him." Though Christ planned to journey to Jerusalem for the Passover, He took time for that beggar. He refused to pass him over. The compassion of Jesus should have convicted His followers who rushed to make progress—a pace that caused them to neglect those who needed His attention.

Those who told Bartimaeus to hush hurried to shift their views. "Cheer up! On your feet! He's calling you," they declared. He heard their words. Again his actions proved his lack of inhibition. He didn't walk with cool composure. He darted to his feet, tossed off his outer garment and raced to Jesus. Childlike faith: displayed in his humble cry, his tenacity, his haste. He refused to waste a second of time. He ran to Jesus.

Do today's followers lack the desperation Bartimaeus possessed? If so, what result shows? Missing the joy of hearing Him say, "Come." Why not push through the obstacles, whether internal or external, and cry for God's help? Those who press through with a cry, who hear His call, just might rush to Jesus with abandon as that beggar did. Instead of strolling leisurely into His presence handicapped by pride or cynicism, the rapid race would be worth the reward. Inundated with anticipation Bartimaeus scurried to the side of the Savior.

How can we understand it? Call it expectant faith. When "the impeding garment is tossed aside, he bounds to his feet. There is a joyous extravagance and recklessness of response, when the soul suddenly becomes responsive to the call of Christ."[6]

THE QUESTION

Jesus then asked the beggar a question. His query seemed unnecessary since the need appeared obvious. Jesus asked, "What do you want me to do?" Why would Christ ask a question as He stared at ample evidence? A blind beggar asked for mercy from a Great Healer. Clearly, he hoped Jesus would cure him of his blindness.

The question is crucial anyway. Again, prayer allows people to participate in the activity of God. He knows all, but has designed His Kingdom so that our asking is often a prerequisite for His working.

View the specific prayer as a key in this design. Communication with God should address real issues. It should stand full of true feeling. Specific needs sent directly to God: call it prayer. Voicing hopes to Him: call it prayer. General "small talk" prayer might cover global ground but often fails to move the heart of the Hearer. Voicing individual needs proves a seriousness. It propels a greater understanding of God's adequacy. It voices desperation toward the One Waiting.

Jesus asked a specific question. He expected an answer. He did not take for granted that the blind man really wanted to see. Maybe he enjoyed his blindness, bitterness and breakdowns so much that he would refuse to cry for deliverance. Some did. Some do. Bartimaeus didn't. He did not want sympathy. He did not crave attention. He did not seek pity that would provide a framework for owning a distinct identity.

Bartimaeus wanted one thing. To be healed. He said, "Rabbi, I want to see." Short. Direct. To the point. That is how to pray. Long litanies overflowing with elegant words? Not required.

Like Bartimaeus, today's prayer requests should be just that. Prayer. Getting to the point. If the mind has no specific words to voice, lingering in God's presence and enjoying Him would be fine. Or letting Him speak. Listening and learning should replace cold-hearted statements.

When needs cover God's people, voices can plead requests to Him. With reverence but without hesitation. With desperation but without elaboration.

Jesus asked. Bartimaeus answered.

THE COMMAND

Jesus then told the beggar to go. He did not give specific direction. He did not announce title, vocation or location. "Be on your way." Christ's command included a benefit, "Your faith has healed you." The text reports an amazing miracle: "Immediately he received his sight and followed Jesus down the road."

Bartimaeus walked in obedience displaying a miracle evident to all. He cried and received a healing. He followed Jesus. The progression dares us to make our requests known to Him.

It also informs us to beware. We might just receive an answer!

What if Bartimaeus had remained in the rut of his begging, never venturing out in faith? What if the crowd's objections deterred him from pursuing Jesus with tenacity? What if he had stopped at any point along the way?

Are we afraid to cry out? Is it hard to admit utter helplessness? Have lifestyles become so entrenched with habit that the thought of losing the norm conquers the apparent Beauty that awaits? What obstacles abort our pursuit? Do memories of unanswered prayers in the past paralyze dreams with doubts?

God says, "Press on!" Pray. Call out to God in desperation. Believe that it can be done and that He is the One who can do it. As you "crash through the quitting points"[7] remember this:

"It is easier for Jesus to give sight to the blind who believe in Him than to make the scales fall from the eyes of His disciples who do not know to what degree they are still blind."[8]

In response to a separate story where a father asked Jesus to heal his epileptic son, Frederick Buechner's comments summarize this chapter. Let his words guide our cries to Jesus.

"What about the boy who is not healed? When, listened to or not listened to, the prayer goes unanswered? Who knows? Just keep praying, Jesus says. Remember the sleepy friend, the crooked judge. Even if the boy dies, keep on beating the path to God's door, because the one thing you can be sure of is that down the path you beat even with your most half-cocked and halting prayer the God you call upon will finally come, and even if he does not bring you the answer you want, he will bring you himself. And maybe at the secret heart of all our prayers that is what we are really praying for."[9]

Beg and plead. Intercede. Those cries are fine. As long as we make sure we direct them toward the Listening Doctor. He, then, can choose to bless beggars like us.

REJOICE that this ministry helps share the Invitation: Tim and Marie Kuck did not let their son Nathaniel's health problems stop them from Inviting others to follow Christ. They also haven't allowed his death to conclude their offers to those begging for help. Their ministry, Nathaniel's Hope, is dedicated in the memory of Nathaniel Timothy Kuck. Its mission is to share the Hope with special needs kids and their families. By encouraging and educating the Christian community to assist in providing respite to families as well as providing resources of encouragement to families with special needs kids, the desire is to see families receive the Hope only Christ can bring. Let them help you. www.NathanielsHope.org

RELEASE your worries by praying, "God, I'm desperate for you."

RECEIVE Christ's Invitation by not displaying energy to impress Him, but displaying energy because you can't live without Him.

RESPOND by Inviting a friend the way Jesus would. Who will you Invite?

RENEW your mind by reading books by Joni Eareckson Tada, C. S. Lewis, Brother Lawrence and Clifton Taulbert.

Chapter 15

A Small Man With a Tall Plan

Jesus entered Jericho and was passing through. A man was there by the name of Zacchaeus; he was a chief tax collector and was wealthy. He wanted to see who Jesus was, but being a short man he could not, because of the crowd. So he ran ahead and climbed a sycamore-fig tree to see him, since Jesus was coming that way.

When Jesus reached the spot, he looked up and said to him, "Zacchaeus, come down immediately. I must stay at your house today." So he came down at once and welcomed him gladly.

All the people saw this and began to mutter, "He has gone to be the guest of a 'sinner.' "

But Zacchaeus stood up and said to the Lord, "Look, Lord! Here and now I give half of my possessions to the poor, and if I have cheated anybody out of anything, I will pay back four times the amount."

Jesus said to him, "Today salvation has come to this house, because this man, too, is a son of Abraham. For the Son of Man came to seek and to save what was lost."[1]

—*Dr. Luke*

> The quest to find personal fulfillment turns on the same mistaken questions: How will it make <u>me</u> feel? How will it make <u>me</u> look?[2]
>
> —Chuck Colson

> Thus conversion is far more than an emotional release and much more than an intellectual adherence to correct doctrine. It is a basic change in life direction.[3]
>
> —Jim Wallis

Years ago I studied this passage only days before embarking on a short vacation. My plans got my attention. The list maker that I am, I jotted notes to myself regarding plans for the trip. My mind jumped from concerns about organizing for ensuring all would be well while I was away, to thoughts about money, the vehicle and other travel arrangements. I was not anxious; I just wanted to be ready.

I have three sons. My oldest two took a much different route in gearing up for the trip. They had no "things-to-do" lists. They looked forward to going, but they felt no hint of concern about any issues crucial to the journey. They planned to go, but they did no planning about going.

Since the trip fell in the middle of holiday season, my boys would be filled with excitement. The night before our departure they would bounce around, unable to conceal their happiness; they would beam with joy from the holiday activities, eager to visit relatives they do not see often. Our baby hardly knew the difference. Other than a lengthy, uncomfortable ride in a car seat, his routine would vary only slightly. The older guys, though? I expected them to sleep restlessly and giggle incessantly as the big day arrived.

My wife and I would be no less enthusiastic, but our joy would manifest itself more in practical preparation than in loud behavior.

A Small Man With a Tall Plan

Anticipation is exhibited differently according to each person's level of maturity. Regardless of the manifestation, anticipation is a powerful force that causes us to look ahead with hope that a good day or a good friend or a good time waits just around the bend. Planning, organizing and carrying out are essential to realizing the dream.

THE PLAN OF ZACCHAEUS

I wonder how Zacchaeus felt when he first learned of Christ's arrival. We do not know how long Zacchaeus knew of the event prior to its occurrence. His eagerness to see Jesus, however, reveals some level of intense anticipation.

News had spread throughout the region. The reputation of Jesus reached far. The audience waited. Some people loved Him; some hated Him. Most seemed unsure about Him. And very curious.

For Zacchaeus, life as usual consisted of a nice income linked to a terrible social life. As the chief tax collector, people enjoyed seeing him show up about as much as a famine. He could pay his bills and have money left over. He headed the district collection of taxes for the Romans with a job that kept food on his table and friends at a distance. Crookedness was as much a part of the vocation as the needed knowledge of accounting.

When this "sawed off little social disaster"[4] heard Jesus was going to be traveling in his direction, he reacted with zeal. He did not have friends or a good reputation, but he knew one thing. Zacchaeus wanted to see the Man he regularly heard about. He wanted to see who Jesus was or what He was or what He could do for him.

Waiting to see Jesus was an admirable desire. We grow sad when people resist even offering Jesus a chance to impact their lives. Longing to see Him, however, is not enough. If the desire does not translate into action that makes the objective possible, what good gets accomplished? Many people dream of a lovely encounter with Jesus that would result in a lifetime relationship with Him, yet they do nothing to make that dream a reality.

Peter had to venture out of a boat onto tumultuous water. Bartimaeus had to cry loudly to be heard above the commotion. Zacchaeus wanted to see Jesus. If he wanted it badly enough, he had to do something about it.

Most of us dream. In our imaginations we write songs, we devise new inventions, we enjoy popularity, we amass great wealth. Dreams do not materialize without effort. The majority of people never advance past the dream stage. Many begin to run out of steam before the finish line.

We can be content with being dreamers or we can become doers. Visualizing yourself speaking another language will not teach you the words of the language. You must take action and endure the labor of learning. Dream of learning to play an instrument? Hard work can turn the dream into a reality. Walking into a bookstore and picturing your name on the cover of a book will not make you an author. Researching, outlining, and pounding out words and paragraphs can. We are all dreamers. Some become doers.

In our spiritual lives we are faced with that choice. We can hope of drawing near to Jesus, but the fulfillment of that hunger will lie dormant until we take action. Zacchaeus' desire to see Jesus began to move toward fulfillment when he took action.

The decisions of Zacchaeus have provided fuel for countless songs and sermons over the years. A short guy climbing a tree to see over the heads of a crowd intrigues us. Discouragement over his stature and the size of a crowd could have derailed the pursuit of his dream. Zacchaeus did not let that stop him; his determination overruled his dilemma. He implemented his plan of seeing Jesus by climbing the now famous sycamore tree.

THE PURPOSE OF CHRIST

Jesus came to seek and save the lost ones.[5] Every encounter we have examined shows Him practicing that strategy. Nothing distracted Jesus from fulfilling the purpose of His coming. He lived and loved with that aim driving His every action and His every word.

A Small Man With a Tall Plan

With Zacchaeus, the purpose of Christ is again revealed clearly. When he reached the spot where Zacchaeus watched from his perch, He looked up to see what must have been a comical sight: a wealthy, friendless, short guy roosting in a tree, determined to see Jesus passing by. The watcher got more than he expected. Notice the words Christ spoke to him:

"Zacchaeus," Jesus chuckles, "What are you doing up there? Isn't it about time for lunch? Come down here on the double. I'll be your guest today."

As a result of those words, two very interesting actions took place. First, Zacchaeus obeyed. Then, we are told, he welcomed Jesus gladly.

Both actions are qualified. The first act—Zac's obedience—occurred with haste. His next act, welcoming Christ while smiling, reveals his attitude. He didn't just receive Jesus because it was expected, nor did Jesus sharply insist that they meet. The small man opened his mind, his heart and his home for Jesus this way: gladly.

The personal contact of Christ shines in this scene. He lived real love in a personal nature. He tackled the enormous task of reaching mankind one person at a time. He did not accost people and demand allegiance from those ignorant of the cause. He touched people individually. Even when he taught large groups, the emphasis of His method leaned on the side of a few.

Jesus drew near people personally, not politically. Remember: He stopped, then glanced at Zacchaeus. A smile on His face. Warmth in His voice. Having Christ's undivided attention, Zac worried about no one else around.

Because Jesus lived in total commitment to His life-purpose, criticism did not control Him. The grumbling was another round of the gripes that by then had grown old: "He has gone to the home of a sinner." Zacchaeus' anticipation contrasted sharply with the condemnation of the crowd. Likewise, their faultfinding is the reverse of the Master's receptivity.

What the critics intended as a complaint, Jesus saw as a compliment, a sign showing He was doing the right thing. They accused Him of doing the very thing He had been given charge to do. His goal? Reach the lost. Jesus did that consistently, giving special attention to each one He received, to each one watching Him take a walk.

The bigotry of the pious grumblers displayed their complete misunderstanding of Christ's purpose. Similar judgmental attitudes can prevail in our days, in our churches, in our minds. A person viewing life through different shades than those we see through? We analyze. A person acting slightly unlike how we conclude they should behave? We criticize.

We sit in our trees. Instead of looking for Jesus, we critique the behavior of all the short men among the limbs. We munch on our preferred Manna without sharing meals with the starving sinners sitting nearby. Meanwhile, Jesus passes without us noticing. In our roles of watching the watchers we miss a chance to climb up to view the Traveler for ourselves.

This story makes the purpose of Jesus clear. His focus? Individuals. Not masses. His plan included multitudes, but He sought to win them one sinner at a time. He stayed true to His reason for being and never allowed the critics to control Him. Today's agenda remains the same.

THE PROCESS OF SALVATION

Many people struggle with this type of story. Jesus welcoming Zacchaeus? It almost removes any need for proper conduct. It almost approves an unethical lifestyle. It almost broadcasts sinners as those who fall under the category of Everything is Really Okay.

Accepting a person who lives in darkness does not equal an endorsement of the behavior that separates them from Safety. It offers a Tour Guide to take them out of their danger zone.

Jesus spent time with sinners. Unlike the legalists, He knew the difference between acceptance and approval. He did not preach a "soft gospel," but neither did He avoid sinners until they ceased to be sinners. He knew that without Him they would remain just as they were. Christ chose to not let that happen.

He accepted them. He loved them just like He found them, loving them enough to offer a proposal of major changes. Great News

A Small Man With a Tall Plan

for them. Then. And for us. Now. As long as we understand our names are listed among the sinners despite our attempts at pretending we belong elsewhere.

So, did Jesus know about Zac's needs before the tree climbing routine? Did God lure us up on a limb before we knew what was actually occurring? Maybe the thought of salvation as a process seems foreign to us. The Bible places our God of Grace as the One who already watches our faces before we begin to seek His.

Zacchaeus longed to see Christ. He took action to make that dream a reality. He ran ahead. He climbed a tree. Jesus acknowledged him and went to Zac's house for a meal. Then, the narrative races forward without giving us the details of that amazing home group meeting. We do notice, though, what Christ's encounter with the tree-climbing man did. It changed his life. Totally.

The short man took a tall turn. We call it repentance. Remember what we have already investigated regarding the journey of conversion. Zac's peeking and climbing, Christ's walking and welcoming; the process was at work. While we view an experience of conversion throughout the Bible, it is neither the beginning nor the end of God's grace at work on a human heart.

Repentance is crucial to conversion. It must not be altered or deleted. No need to neglect it. No need to subtract it from sermons to soften the blow. No need to turn it into a mere emotional release containing no future effect on behavior. Coming to Christ includes crossing the bridge of repentance. No other route can take us there. Still not sure? Ask the Old Testament prophets to answer your questionnaire. Beam a note to John the Baptist. Give Jesus a call and get His view. Take a long walk with early Christians who died preaching a message of repentance.[6]

How can we really understand it? In his book, *Call to Conversion*, Jim Wallis gives a definition of repentance:

> "Our word repentance conjures up feelings of being sorry or guilty for something. The biblical meaning is far deeper and richer. In the New Testament usage, repentance is the essential first step to conversion. In the larger rhythm of turning from and turning to, repentance is the turning away

from....We turn from all that binds and oppresses us and others, from all the violence and evil in which we are so complicit, from all the false worship that has controlled and corrupted us. Ultimately, repentance is turning from the powers of death."[7]

Four aspects work in the drama of repentance:

- Recognition: "I have wronged."
- Remorse: "I am sorry."
- Redirection: "I want to turn away from sin and toward the Savior."
- Restitution: "I will right what wrongs I can."

Add those four Rs together and what does it equal? Repentance. We have mentioned it. We have noticed Christ's clear, and often confusing, communication of turning from and turning toward.

Some of those are evident in this chapter's story. Others are implied. Zac recognized his condition. He felt bad enough to do something about it. Whatever words came out in his conversation with Jesus, the result was a redirection of that man's life.

> "Zacchaeus was so taken aback by the honor of the thing that before he had a chance to change his mind, he promised not only to turn over fifty percent of his holdings to the poor but to pay back, four to one, all the cash he'd extorted from everybody else. Jesus was absolutely delighted."[8]

Repentance turned Zac in the right direction. What can we learn? Maybe "recognizing our own helpless dependence and accepting that we are blind, naked beggars in need of sight. Then it is possible for us after receiving our sight, to follow him on the Way. Repentance is a painful experience, for it feels humiliating, but it is the first step towards the wholeness which Jesus promises us."[9]

Sound good?

Let's not allow familiarity with the story to diminish the impact our hearts desires. I'm a little Zac, too. Aren't you? In that turn of

A Small Man With a Tall Plan

events, in that great turn of life, everything hinged on that man seeking Jesus. The Savior sought Him, but responded as Zac climbed high enough to take a courageous glance. Would the Master's wish have been thwarted if the tree had not become a peeking place?

If we need to see Jesus better, let's do whatever we must to gain a glance. No inconvenience is too tall, no ability too short.

Climb a tree. Bend a knee. Close eyes. Open ears. Sing a song. Whisper a prayer. Turn from sin. See the Savior.

He is passing by. Don't let Him travel through without stopping by our place for lunch. Salvation is the best meal to order.

REJOICE that this ministry helps share the Invitation: James Dobson's name doesn't sound new to most of us. But, how does he help us climb up to learn, then let Jesus come to our homes? Let Focus on the Family help you hear Christ's Invitation to your house.
www.family.org

One family I watched serve Jesus together through the years is now Inviting the world in a variety of ways. Les and Dianne Hall worked with me on staff for a long time. Dianne helped type and edit my first draft of Beggars. Les helped me and our church in so many ways. Their daughter Stephanie, and their son and daughter-in-law Jeremy and Melissa, all shine examples of Christ's Invitations. Pray for them and send them a note as they work with an international missions agency focused on development and training in Central Asia: halll@ahope.org, halljm@galacticomm.org, halls@galacticomm.org

RELEASE your worries by praying, "God, give me the courage to climb up today and get a new glimpse at Jesus."

RECEIVE Christ's Invitation by going to a place you have never been and picturing Christ Inviting Himself to your house. Imagine taking Him home.

RESPOND by Inviting a friend the way Jesus would. Who will you Invite?

RENEW your mind by reading books by James Dobson, Ed Silvoso, Dutch Sheets, Francis Frangipane and Kathleen Norris.

Chapter 16

DRESSED FOR SUCCESS

Jesus spoke to them again in parables, saying: "The kingdom of heaven is like a king who prepared a wedding banquet for his son. He sent his servants to those who had been invited to the banquet to tell them to come, but they refused to come.

"Then he sent some more servants and said, 'Tell those who have been invited that I have prepared my dinner: My oxen and fattened cattle have been butchered, and everything is ready. Come to the wedding banquet.'

"But they paid no attention and went off—one to his field, another to his business. The rest seized his servants, mistreated them and killed them. The king was enraged. He sent his army and destroyed those murderers and burned their city.

"Then he said to his servants, 'The wedding banquet is ready, but those I invited did not deserve to come. Go to the street corners and invite to the banquet anyone you find.' So the servants went out into the streets and gathered all the people they could find, both good and bad, and the wedding hall was filled with guests.

> "But when the king came in to see the guests, he noticed a man there who was not wearing wedding clothes. 'Friend,' he asked, 'how did you get in here without wedding clothes?' The man was speechless.
>
> "Then the king told the attendants, 'Tie him hand and foot, and throw him outside, into the darkness, where there will be weeping and gnashing of teeth.'
>
> "For many are invited, but few are chosen."[1]
>
> —*Matthew*

> We try to soften hell and some even seek to deny it. Jesus, however, does not allow for this conclusion.[2]
>
> —*Dr. John H. Gerstner*

> Many will say to me on that day, "Lord, Lord, did we not prophesy in your name, and in your name drive out demons and perform many miracles?" Then I will tell them plainly, "I never knew you. Away from me, you evildoers!"[3]
>
> —*Jesus, the Son of God*

What are you wearing? I'm not trying to be too personal, but admit it. The clothes we wear reveal much about us. Fashions we refuse to support and attitudes about dress codes and unexpected comments by observers noticing too many wrinkles in our too-often worn shirt: What motives steer us and what emotions stir us? Do we choose wardrobes more for comfort enjoyed or statements made? Do our styles indicate desires to conform and fit in, or to resist and stand out? Do fashion expenditures tip the balance of our budgets or do we remain within the confines of income without fears of others' opinions? Do clothes really make the man or woman? Can we really dress to insure success?

Don't panic. This chapter isn't a treatise on fashion flaws or dress code standards. Neither is it an expose' on the perils of a society dominated by an industry. The text motivates me to ask. In this parable, we observe a scenario where choice of apparel is not optional, where one found to be improperly dressed faces severe consequences. We see those refusing to dress properly for a special occasion, and how they failed to dress for success.

As with most of His parables, Jesus told this story in response to a problem. Too often we attempt to decipher the meaning behind parables without first gaining a clear understanding of the issue He addressed. We can remove an illustration from the context of a sermon and still have a good, solid illustration. We could use it one way one time, and another way a different time, by stressing a portion of the picture. An illustration about rain could emphasize seasonal patterns, incorrect predictions, dangerous dryness, or an umbrella's protection. Parables, however, must not be forced to shift where they belong. To make it do so would leave us with a good story, but one removed from its intended purpose. Parables make points.

A PROBLEM

Christ told His parables to get people's attention in order to tell them something. But, He allowed the parables themselves to do the telling. As He responded to questions or troublesome issues, He verbally drew pictures for the investigators to notice. Frequently, Pharisees were the ones asking, debating, investigating.

Oh, the Pharisees. We've encountered them often in the journey through the Invitations of Jesus. They maintained morality outwardly while neglecting internal spirituality. They believed with confidence they had the corner in the truth market. Their external ethics, surface conformity and rigid traditionalism presented an impressive show of religion. Their sincerity and success listed them as masters of their game. They comprised the God Squad: determined to please God and purge Israel of the uncommitted.

They look a lot like me.

To gain an accurate picture of the dilemma facing Jesus, let's keep this parable in its proper place. Here is the play-by-play of events recorded in Matthew 21:

- Jesus entered Jerusalem riding on a donkey. "The Triumphal Entry" included cloaks spread across the ground, palm branches waved high, and shouts of "Hosanna."
- Jesus walked into the temple and angrily drove out the merchants, overturning tables and cracking a hand-made whip. He rebuked religious materialists for turning God's House of Prayer into a Den of Robbers.
- Jesus left Jerusalem and spent the night in Bethany. On the way back into the city Jesus spotted a fig tree and hoped to ease His hunger by eating a fig. Finding nothing but leaves, He cursed the fig tree. The tree withered immediately.
- Jesus reached the city and began teaching in the temple. Chief priests and elders questioned His authority.
- Jesus told the story of two sons whose father instructed them to go into a field and work for the day. The first son refused. Later, he changed his mind and went. The second son agreed to go, but never made it to the field. Jesus used the story as a springboard to proclaim to Jewish leaders that sinners could enter the Kingdom ahead of them.
- Jesus told them another story. This time He spoke of a landowner who rented his vineyard to farmers who killed servants sent by the owner to gather the harvest. Jesus allowed the elders to make His point for Him when they concluded that the owner would "bring those wretches to a wretched end." Christ's point again was that the ones initially entrusted with the Truth would be tossed out in favor of those sincerely accepting the Truth.

That series of events baffled the Jewish leaders. Jesus accused them of rejecting Yahweh, no small charge for career-driven religious leaders. Hearing that Jesus of Nazareth believed a prostitute could enter the Kingdom at all made them shudder. But, when He said the hookers just might go ahead of, or instead of, a chief priest, His words had hit the blasphemy phase. Notice their response:

> "When the chief priests and Pharisees heard Jesus' parables, they knew he was talking about them. They looked for a way to arrest him, but they were afraid of the crowd because the people held he was a prophet."[4]

The Pharisee tradition convinced them God was on their side. Self-righteousness reinforced their dependence on outward pickiness instead of inner piety. Rooted in pride, they heard Christ's words and realized they were the target. But, they couldn't fathom the possibility that He might be right. Their eyes were blind and their hearts were hard.

Again, I notice myself.

To address the Pharisee's rejection of the very God they loved, Jesus told a story to draw attention to that rejection. A study of the story omitting that context neglects the key that unlocks Christ's meaning. We must observe the problem in order to understand the parable. Even if it reminds us of us.

A PARABLE

Like a heavyweight fighter Jesus had the Pharisees reeling. He packed His stinging punches with Truth. He powered them by Justice. The Pharisees staggered, though remaining oblivious to this fact: God hoped to get their attention and win back their hearts. Not to His image. To Him. Not to His rules. To Him.

Instead of falling to their knees in surrender, they ran to their corners and hoped to devise a strategy to knock out their formidable foe.

When the bell rang and began the next round, Jesus didn't back down. He remained with His plan. He continued to jab away with parables. He delivered a right hook with the frightening smack of the "Parable of a Wedding Banquet."

This story deserves a place among the Invitations of Jesus. It captures the intriguing summary of separating those who will enter from those who will remain outside.

Go back to the opening page of this chapter. Reread Matthew's account of the parable. Then, compare it with a similar story from Luke's version. I include it here. Together they express a strong message.

Jesus replied: "A certain man was preparing a great banquet and invited many guests. At the time of the banquet he sent his servant to tell those who had been invited, 'Come, for everything is now ready.'

"But they all alike began to make excuses. The first said, 'I have just bought a field, and I must go and see it. Please excuse me.'

"Another said, 'I have just bought five yoke of oxen, and I'm on my way to try them out. Please excuse me.'

"Still another said, 'I just got married, so I can't come.'

"The servant came back and reported this to his master. Then the owner of the house became angry and ordered his servant, 'Go out quickly into the streets and alleys of the town and bring in the poor, the crippled, the blind and the lame.'

" 'Sir,' the servant said, 'what you ordered has been done, but there is still room.'

"Then the master told his servant, 'Go out to the roads and country lanes and make them come in, so that my house will be full. I tell you, not one of those men who were invited will get a taste of my banquet.' "[5]

While the two stories are similar, they also differ. I include Luke's account to stress the point of separation and to show that gospel writers all knew that Jesus taught of not only love and peace, but also of impending doom.

Going back to our original focus, "The Wedding Banquet," we should understand that the story presents a common event in the ancient world. The wedding celebration was a big happening. Rejecting an Invitation to such a banquet implied rejection of the Inviter who had gone to much expense to provide a delightful experience for all who attended.

It was also part of the oriental custom to present a festival robe

Dressed for Success

to each guest invited to the royal feast.[6] So, as Jesus told His story, the hearers could relate. That is one of the features of parables; they were believable.

A POINT

Remember, the parables emphasize one major point. I am tempted to allegorize them and force a spiritual application out of every factor in the story. More than one factor may possess enormous meaning, but what Jesus meant is all we really need here. Instead of forcing words into them, let's allow them to speak to us.

The clinching phrase is the concluding one:
"For many are invited, but few are chosen."

The king who organized his son's wedding banquet invited many friends. When the many Invited ones showed their disinterest, the Invitation was extended to include anyone they could find who would agree to come.

When the king found a man in the meeting hall without the proper clothing—the robe they gave to all who accepted the Invitation—he became angry. He had the man tossed out. The point? The Invitation had gone to many, but only those wearing the robe to prove acceptance were allowed to remain. Those attempting to participate without the proper attire were not chosen, even if they had been among those initially Invited.

The imagery of darkness, weeping and gnashing of teeth paints a terrifying picture. Is there proof elsewhere in Scripture that a horrible fate awaits those who die without admission to the Kingdom's wedding banquet?

- When the disciples asked Jesus if only a few would be saved, His answer included a reference to a place of weeping and gnashing of teeth that is reserved for those the Doorman does not know.[7]
- Jesus frequently referred to hell and pain as the destiny for those dying without the Truth.[8]

Historically, Christians have believed in the reality of hell. Notice the strong words from Jonathan Edwards' classic sermon, "Sinners in the Hands of An Angry God":

> "The wrath of God burns against them, their damnation does not slumber; the pit is prepared, the fire is made ready, the furnace is now hot, ready to receive them; the flames do now rage and glow. The glittering sword is whet, and held over them, and the pit hath opened its mouth under them."[9]

How can we avoid such a hellish destination? By entering the banquet wearing proper clothing. What is that clothing? The righteousness of Christ. Not of us, our system, our institution or our routine.

Morality isn't the robe allowing acceptance at the feast. Godly parents cannot clothe us, nor can church attendance or mission trips or seminary degrees. Good tradition, good training or good trying might score points on earth. But, they don't Invite or clothe us for the banquet. Accepting the Invitation of Jesus and wearing His robe of righteousness is the only hope.

Each attendee must arrive dressed properly or risk facing expulsion.

The Invitation? Grace.
The acceptance? Faith.
The clothing? The righteousness of Christ.
All so clothed will be chosen.
How about us? Are we dressed for eternal success?

REJOICE that this ministry helps share the Invitation: Experts told Larry Myers he was too old to leave his role as a pastor and venture into missions work. The Inviter told Larry and Mary Lou to go. They did. Now, Mexico Ministries continues offering ministry, medical help and construction work to Beggars in waiting. I've been there with Larry. He has taken me places where natives don't wear clothes, where they had never seen people like us and where they needed us to tell them about Jesus. Hundreds of churches have been built. Through his schools and medical clinics, Larry trains nationals and allows them to Invite whosoever will come. Ask how you can help: mexicoministries@msn.com

I would also encourage you to rejoice about the ministry of Fellowship of Christian Athletes. Find out how you can support their ministry in your area: www.fca.org

RELEASE your worries by praying, "God, forgive me for trying to impress you."

RECEIVE Christ's Invitation by falling in love with Him again.

RESPOND by Inviting a friend the way Jesus would. Who will you Invite?

RENEW your mind by reading James Watkins, Bill Hybels, Andrew Murray, John Bevere, R. C. Sproul and Bruce Wilkinson.

Chapter 17

DOES ANYBODY KNOW WHAT TIME IT IS?

"At that time the kingdom of heaven will be like ten virgins who took their lamps and went out to meet the bridegroom. Five of them were foolish and five were wise. The foolish ones took their lamps but did not take any oil with them. The wise, however, took oil in jars along with their lamps. The bridegroom was a long time in coming, and they all became drowsy and fell asleep.

"At midnight the cry rang out: 'Here's the bridegroom! Come out to meet him!'

"Then all the virgins woke up and trimmed their lamps. The foolish ones said to the wise, 'Give us some of your oil; our lamps are going out.'

" 'No,' they replied, 'there may not be enough for both us and you. Instead, go to those who sell oil and buy some for yourselves.'

"But while they were on their way to buy the oil, the bridegroom arrived. The virgins who were ready went in with him to the wedding banquet. And the door was shut.

"Later the others also came. 'Sir! Sir!' they said. 'Open the door for us!'

"But he replied, 'I tell you the truth, I don't know you.'

"Therefore keep watch, because you do not know the day or the hour.[1]

—Jesus, as recorded in Matthew's account

There's a slow, slow train coming,
Coming 'round the bend.[2]

—Bob Dylan

88 Reasons Why the Rapture Will Be in 1988[3]
—Book Title by author
Edgar Whisenant

A popular song from my younger days asked if anybody really knew what time it was. It then asked if anybody really cared.[4] With regard to days and months, hours and minutes, I answer yes to both questions. Most of the time we know what time it is. Some of the time we care, really.

In fact, many of us live our lives driven by a time fixation. The obsession dominates and dictates. A malfunctioning watch around my wrist leaves me abandoned. I take it seriously, like I'm lost at sea with no bearings. During a recent sabbatical, God instructed me to become free from my addiction. He told me to take off my watch and leave home without it. We argued. He won. I survived.

Concern about time isn't all that bad, though. Existence within the box of time necessitates a certain awareness. Occupations, expectations and conscientiousness demand operation according to rules. Time ranks high among that guide. We really do care what time it is.

But, Scripture informs us that time will eventually cease to govern us. Its Creator will screech its rule to a sudden stop. Regarding the permanence of time, none of us really knows what time it is, or when days and hours no longer exist in their present form. Jesus, according to the Bible, will return to earth to exchange the status quo for a new model of Kingdom living.

In light of that eternal truth, what time is it now? We wonder when. We wonder how. Questions cloak our thoughts of time's conclusion. But, do we really care what time it is on eternity's calendar? I'm not sure. I'm sure of this, though: I see mixed signals in myself. Discussions of time's end stir curiosity, but inquisitiveness falls short of actual concern if it never translates into action.

I think and I blink. I evaluate and debate. Then, I check the time on my Palm Pilot and rush to be where I'm going fifteen minutes before the listed appointment. Eternity came and left my brain cells in a hurry.

Sermons. Seminars. Lectures. Books. When eschatology is the subject, interest rises. Want to draw a crowd? Plan an end-time emphasis. Promise charts, graphs, dates. People will show. But, what good will it do us if lives remain unchanged. Maybe we notice signs while ignoring solutions. Crowds love the topic, not the Truth. Excitement doesn't necessarily equal commitment. Eschatological voyeurism is not Christianity.

Every generation has wondered if life as it is would dissolve. And, if so, when? And, if so, what would be left? The comments of Christ from chapters 24 and 25 of Matthew's Gospel address the end of time. Inquisitive disciples, sparked by the anxiety of not knowing those answers, asked Jesus to clue them in on the signs signifying the end of the age.[5]

Jesus answered their question with a lengthy treatment known as the Olivet Discourse. The title comes from its delivery from the Mount of Olives. Jesus used facts, illustrations, instructions, historical examples, prophecies and parables. One parable, often called "The Parable of the Ten Virgins," serves as this chapter's text. The story contrasts most of our Invitations. I've included it because of my firm conviction that Jesus longs compassionately for us to follow Him beyond time. He yearns for our presence. I feel awed and humble as I attempt to comprehend that.

So, the Invitation "Come out to meet him,"[6] travels from a cultural story into the hunger of human hearts who wonder of time's end, and who need the Time Maker to transform questions into confidence. He wants us now and forever. His Invitation is permanent. His instructions flow clearly in this parable. I hope to heed its sober call.

The parable paints a picture of Christ's return, using the setting of an oriental wedding. Ten young girls, eager to meet the bridegroom and join the processional to greet his bride, decided they needed torches to light the way and escort the groom properly. To keep the torches lit, oil was required to soak the rags that would burn on the torch ends. No specific time had been announced as to when the groom would arrive and call for them. He delayed his coming. The girls grew weary. Eventually each of them fell asleep.

When the call of his impending arrival came forth, the startled escorts scrambled, gathering themselves and their provisions. Five of the girls had torches, but no oil. The other young ladies had prepared in advance for that moment. They possessed an adequate supply of oil for the procession.

What did the others do? They begged for oil, but their requests were denied. Forced to go out and purchase oil, the foolish virgins missed the groom's arrival. In attempting to get into the wedding banquet later, the foolish girls found the door closed and the groom unwilling to let them enter.

FIVE WISE VIRGINS

All ten of the girls had fallen asleep. All hoped of joining the procession, assuming a place at the wedding banquet.

> "What differentiates the foolish from the wise is precisely the failure of the former to face the possibility that the bridegroom, their returning Lord, may come earlier or later than they expect, and that in any case the coming will be so sudden that it will afford no opportunity for making good deficiencies which are then discovered."[7]

Unlike their foolish counterparts, the girls labeled as wise saw the importance of preparation. They all began with anticipation and enthusiasm. Only the wise, though, made sure their excitement translated into constructive behavior. They secured the needed oil. Because of their foresight and readiness, the call, "Here is the bridegroom," was a pleasant and welcoming Invitation.

When we speak of Christ's return, we frequently speak of its occurrence using the biblical phrase, "as a thief in the night."[8] The apostle Paul, however, wrote to the Thessalonian believers that the day shouldn't "surprise" Christians the way a thief would.[9] He does not imply that we know the date of Christ's coming. His point is that we know the fact of His return and that our knowledge causes us to live in a state of readiness. Though the day comes like a thief in the night, we do not need to be totally caught off guard.

How, then, can we act out the role of the wise virgins? How should we live so that His coming does not surprise us? What practical action insures that our supply of oil meets the requirement? Paul admonished his readers about maintaining readiness:

1. Be alert and self-controlled
2. Put on faith and love as a breastplate
3. Put on the hope of salvation as a helmet
4. Encourage and build one another up[10]

Alertness and self-control go together. They refer to attitudes and actions, not emotions. Both words are in the present subjunctive mood, which indicates continuous action or an ongoing state of being. What this means to us is the alertness and self-control that should describe the lifestyles of people who follow Jesus must be ongoing, continuous, never ceasing.

Regardless of whether or not we feel ready or steady, we must act in an awareness of the Kingdom, yielding to the Spirit's authority. Alertness signifies a state of being wide-awake. Self-control indicates remaining free from "every form of mental and spiritual 'drunkenness'," and to be well-balanced, free from any excesses, temperate and clear-headed.[11]

I've watched the World Series many times. Growing up in

Georgia, I've pulled for the Braves. Years ago, I watched my most exciting series and it wasn't the Braves. I wasn't even tempted to fall asleep at my usual early-to-bed time. My brother-in-law played. Even when I felt tired, I was filled with expectation. It gave me the desire to stay awake.

I started 2003 watching my oldest son's band play Christian rock. Listening to loud music on a stormy night when my doctors want an epileptic, seizure-prone guy like me to get to bed? Hey, it was my son Taylor and his friends.

Christians who live with an expectancy of Christ's return resist the tendency to shut their spiritual eyes. Too much is at stake. Alertness is crucial.

Want to be prepared for the Bridegroom? Be wide-awake and clear headed.

Next, we are to put on faith and love as a breastplate. The breastplate protects us against injury to vital organs. Faith and love teamwork as the armor surrounding and protecting us, keeping us spiritually alive. Again, actions. Not just emotions. Faith: a belief wedded to behavior. Love, though a distorted concept in our sensually obsessed society, may be accompanied by warm feelings of attraction. But not necessarily. Love means displaying behavior to better the life of the person loved.

No one always feels full of faith. No one always feels full of love. The beauty of relying on God's guidance instead of our skills is that God enables us to supernaturally do what we don't have the desire or the power to do.[12] We can, through God, prepare for Christ's return by protecting our spiritual vitality with faith and love.

Paul continued his armor imagery with his next admonition: Put on the hope of salvation as a helmet. Our minds can be protected by hope. As life gets tough, many people falter spiritually. Been there? Done that? Past disappointments and present discouragements clamp around us like a vice. Restricted, we often fail by stopping our progress. Where is the battlefield? The mind.

I know thoughts of hope should prevail in us. The battle tricks us, though. Let us remember—today—that while frustration and failure are inevitable, they aren't invincible. Depression attacks indiscriminately, but we can overcome. Sadness camps in our land, but we must never allow it to dominate. Hope can overrule hopelessness. Even at the worst of times.

Paul qualified hope. He recommended a specific type of hope. For our outlooks to become positive, salary increases and safe travel and scenic vacations don't cause that desired effect. Christ's return does. It represents the ultimate rescue.

This doesn't promote an escapist mentality. Far from it. It means we mentally refuse to allow the darkness of daily lives to dispel the light of eternal life. Because He will come for us, our lives here and now take on new and ultimate meaning. Remember: "God did not appoint us to wrath but to receive salvation through our Lord Jesus Christ."[13]

We prepare by encouraging and building up one another. Admit it. We need improvement. We are too quick to judge, to condemn, to tear down. We are too careless with our words, too cautious with our acceptance. These New Testament passages reveal the roles encouragement and edification can have. Reading them reminds me of a standard to pursue.

"Accept him whose faith is weak, without passing judgement on disputable matters."

"Let us therefore make every effort to do what leads to peace and to mutual edification."

"We who are strong ought to bear with the failings of the weak and not to please ourselves. Each of us should please his neighbor for his good, to build him up."

"Accept one another, then, just as Christ accepted you, in order to bring praise to God."[14]

Reading 1 Corinthians 13 helps...after it hurts. Applying 1 Corinthians 13 heals. After it convicts. Readying ourselves for Christ's return by loving others; let's call it Christianity. Like the wise virgins who welcomed the groom's arrival by preparing, implementing these ethics increases our supply of oil as we eagerly await His next visit.

FIVE FOOLISH VIRGINS

The beauty of this parable is tempered by the bitterness of the full story. For the five remaining girls, expectation ended in tragedy. They faced the pathetic consequences of their procrastination. Because they made no provision for the bridegroom's delay, the door closed, banning their entry permanently.

> "The haunting pathos of the late-comers finding the door closed in their faces was caught and expressed by Tennyson in the song, 'Late, late, so late! and dark the night and chill?' which was sung to Guinevere by the little maid in the nunnery where the queen had sought sanctuary....They hammered on the street-door and shouted to the door-keeper, 'O Sir! O Sir! please let us in'. But all the answer they received was 'No, I don't know you'. So they had to go back home in the dark, tired and disappointed, because they had not been ready."[15]

Throughout these Invitations of Jesus we have seen His tenderness and compassion. Even in His sternness, His kindness pours forth from His words and His touch.[16] Our view of the compassionate Christ must, however, never compromise the inevitable consequences facing those who reject the Savior. Soon, midnight falls. When He interrupts our lives to birth a new day, the door of opportunity closes. Those unprepared remain outside. They can never get in.

I think of how people often gear up for hurricanes here in Florida. The first few times I heard of coastal cities taking necessary precautions, I was ready to prepare. When little damage came my way, I didn't think too much about it the next time. Scary, isn't it?

Spiritually, we grow deaf to warnings of the final storm. That Day approaches. Only those in a state of readiness will welcome it. Others, like the foolish virgins, will face the Day unprepared. The outcome? They will "seek death, but will not find it; they will long to die, but death will elude them."[17]

ONE DAY SOON

When, we often ask, will it be? That is part of the great mystery. We believe Jesus is coming, but we don't know when. Many have predicted His arrival and all have watched their faces turn red as the dates came and left without His return. Large groups have sold homes to wait atop a mountain in anticipation of a coming that never came.

Remember Y-2K? I argued with people, many people much more intelligent than I can even pretend to be. They felt convinced about that date's disaster. I doubted them.

Date setters will continue to be wrong. As big days pass uneventfully, experts scramble to reevaluate their data and readjust their dates. No matter. They will still be wrong.

For this chapter's eschatological inspection, I have no dispensational timetables, earthquake counts or possible dates. I pray for Israel, but carry no memos in my Palm Pilot to alert me about the latest wars and rumors of wars. I gladly leave that to others who sincerely present scenarios. The experts are many and their books are numerous. I'm not one of them. I learn from them while believing today's guesses will fall far short of what ultimately occurs.[18]

But, will Doubting Chris refuse to prepare for Christ's return? I pray I'm ready and waiting. I pray I'm not alone. I pray the house is packed.

So, while not knowing it all, let's study Revelation and Daniel. As Jesus instructed, let's notice the signs preceding His coming. Refusing to be like those leaders who see themselves as the only ones really knowing how it will happen, let's joyfully await Christ's return.

Jesus can't be reduced to maps, charts and graphs. When He steps foot on this place, He will not only shatter sin, but will also smile at those longing for His arrival.

We must not try to tame Him or cage Him. He's too big.

We must not try to delay our preparation. He wants us with Him.

We must remember to be ready, to keep watch, though we won't have the day pasted on our day-timer.[19]

Are we ready?

Jesus is returning. This time He won't be wrapped in swaddling clothes, but will wield a "sharp sword with which to strike down the nations."[20] This time He won't ride a donkey, but will race ahead on a white horse. The Crucified becomes the Conqueror. The Gentle Man becomes a Judge. No manger and some wise men. This time, His Majesty and His Wisdom.

Jesus is returning. I want us to be among those seated at the banquet table with the Glorious Groom. Am I ready? Are you ready? What about those nearby: our family, our friends, our foes?

Now is the time to purchase the oil.

REJOICE that many colleges help share the Invitation: I attended Emmanuel College in Franklin Springs, GA many years ago. They educate and also train students to Invite people to Jesus (www.emmanuel-college.edu). So does Southeastern College in Lakeland, FL (www.secollege.edu). Mark Rutland, one of my favorite preachers, is their president. Check out the websites of those schools, challenge students to consider attending those or similar schools, pray for Christian schools and colleges in your city and around the world, pray for Christians in every school and college, and support ministries like Chi Alpha (www.chialpha.com) as they seek to reach the world.

RELEASE your worries by praying, "God, help me wait no longer for you."

RECEIVE Christ's Invitation by glancing at a clock. Think about time running out and be grateful you belong to Him.

RESPOND by Inviting a friend the way Jesus would. Who will you Invite?

RENEW your mind by reading books by J. Keith Miller, Corrie ten Boom, Mark Rutland, Brennan Manning and Dr. Henry Cloud & Dr. John Townsend.

Chapter 18

SPENDING THE NIGHT

Then Jesus went with his disciples to a place called Gethsemane, and he said to them, "Sit here while I go over there and pray." He took Peter and the two sons of Zebedee along with him, and he began to be sorrowful and troubled. Then he said to them, "My soul is overwhelmed with sorrow to the point of death. Stay here and keep watch with me."

Going a little farther, he fell with his face to the ground and prayed, "My Father, if it is possible, may this cup be taken from me. Yet not as I will, but as you will."

Then he returned to his disciples and found them sleeping. "Could you men not keep watch with me for one hour?" he asked Peter. "Watch and pray so that you will not fall into temptation. The spirit is willing, but the body is weak."

He went away a second time and prayed, "My Father, if it is not possible for this cup to be taken away unless I drink it, may your will be done."

When he came back, he again found them sleeping, because their eyes were heavy. So he left them and went away once more and prayed the third time, saying the same thing.

Then he returned to the disciples and said to them, "Are you still sleeping and resting? Look, the hour is near, and the Son of Man is betrayed into the hands of sinners. Rise, let us go! Here comes my betrayer!"[1]
—*Matthew*

Humanity is fickle. They may dress for a morning coronation and never feel the need to change clothes to attend an execution in the afternoon.

So Triumphal Sundays and Good Fridays always fit comfortably into the same April week.[2]
—*Calvin Miller*

Prayer catapults us onto the frontier of the spiritual life. It is original research in unexpected territory. Meditation introduces us to the inner life, fasting is an accompanying means, but it is the Discipline of prayer itself that brings us into the deepest and highest work of the human spirit.[3]
—*Richard Foster*

He walked on the water.
He took the hand of a dead girl and lifted her to life.
He fed thousands,
yet always made time for the few.
the people loved Him and hated Him.
marching through life,
propelled by Love,
filled with Truth,
radiating Glory,
Jesus edged ever closer to His death
with each holy step.
by caring for sinners and confronting saints

Spending the Night

He left detractors little option;
they could erase Him or exalt Him,
they could give their lives to Him
or discover a way to take away His.

that night, the drama of His destiny began beating.
loudly. close.
hearing its relentless cadence,
His inner world grew dark;
darker than the unusually dark world around Him
on this night.
yes, He was God.
yes, He was man.
He knew
of the purpose, of the plan.
yet, He felt.
He felt deeply.
maybe to help relieve His pain,
maybe to help them learn to feel true pain,
He invited His disciples.
so many Invitations,
but this one was unique.
He called them,
these He had experienced life with
for three adventurous years,
He called them
to the garden.
deeper into darkness.
deeper into His pain.
deep in prayer with His Father.

then, He called three to go all the way with Him:
peter.
james.
john.
He invited them to agony.
not joy.

Not to gratification and gain.
to emptiness, to loneliness.
troubled, full of sorrow, He walked.
this God-Man looked, sounded,
much more man,
much less God.
voicing His pain in candid words,
His honesty kicked all pretensions aside,
admitting sorrow,
deathlike sorrow,
overwhelmed Him.
He invited three to stay with Him,
speaking like a needy man,
rather than a needed man.
they were to keep watch,
to remain alert,
to give Him that moment.

He went farther into the dark heart of gethsemane
and fell face-first in desperation.
He cried to Father
and asked for reprieve:
"maybe there is another way.
must I drink of the bitter cup?"
the words carried His brokenness, His turmoil;
they proved His pathos.
Jesus did not stop with His desire;
He refused to conclude after sobbing out His hope
for an alternative.
"no matter, God, I will do as You see fit.
carry out Your plan."

He rose from prayer,
from blood, from sweat,
and returned to His watchmen.
He had given them a privileged charge.
He found them sleeping.

Spending the Night

He called them.
He coddled them, taught them, trained them.
then He needed them
in a different way
but they slept.
to peter, who was out like a rock,
He offered a rebuke
tempered only by His exhaustion.
"an hour isn't so much, is it?
only one hour and you cannot
watch with me,
watch for me?
temptation will rob you unless you learn to watch and pray.
the battle rages;
flesh so weak and spirit strong.
feed your spirit.
do not satisfy the flesh."

a second time He cried to God in prayer.
speaking the same words.

a second time He returned.
a second time He found His closest friends sleeping.

a third time He cried to God in prayer.
speaking the same words.

a third time He returned.
a third time He found His closest friends sleeping.

how sad.
their sleepy refusal to spend the night in prayer
when the Master solicited their participation.
didn't they sense His hurt?
didn't they?

they didn't

fight off sleep to embrace prayer, to share pain.
was it could not or would not?
am I different?
what replaces my prayer
as sleep did theirs?

Jesus invited them to pray in the dark.
they slept.
they never liked His talk of death anyway.
maybe a restless nap
helped them escape the nagging awareness
that He really was going away
soon.

years have passed since that dark night.
maybe He weeps even now at God's right hand.
no tears in heaven?
can He see the child slapped by an impatient parent,
the man battling an incurable disease,
the family on the brink of collapse,
the killing of the innocent,
the laughter of the guilty,
the multitudes unmoved by His love?

can He see?
if He sees, He cries.
if He cries, He prays.

always interceding.

if He sees and cries and prays,
He calls us.
He invites us into the darkness of the garden.

spend the night with Him in crucial prayer.
not
pleading for trinkets or hoping for fun.

now,
crying for Life and dying for Love.

tonight,
with the drum of destiny beating, beating, beating,
close and clear,
can we watch one hour?
a bitter cup and a Father's will,
temptation and tears, flesh and spirit.

at this time He cries out to God in prayer.
at some time He will return.

will He find us sleeping?

REJOICE that this ministry helps share the Invitation: House of Hope is a non-denominational, not-for-profit Christian residential program for troubled boys and girls ages 14-17. This work is based upon Biblical principles, proven to provide both workable and successful solutions in restoring troubled teens and their families, resulting in these teens becoming solid citizens and effective, contributing members of society. National House of Hope provides training, consulting, guidance in resource development and serves as a communications network in the establishment of Houses of Hope by citizens, churches and faith-based organizations in local communities.

Through national awareness, guidance and training, while building on the strength and momentum of a local model, National House of Hope is working toward its vision to have a House of Hope within driving distance of every major city in America by 2010. House of Hope maintains a 95% success rate for helping hurting teenagers and restoring families. www.nationalhouseofhope.org

RELEASE your worries by praying, "God, forgive me for not praying with Jesus."

RECEIVE Christ's Invitation by going somewhere different and praying a prayer of desperation.

RESPOND by Inviting a friend the way Jesus would. Who will you Invite?

RENEW your mind by reading books by Walter Wangerin, Anne LaMott and Calvin Miller.

Chapter 19

MAKING RESERVATIONS: HOW TO WAKE IN A WONDERFUL PLACE

One of the criminals who hung there hurled insults at him: "Aren't you the Christ? Save yourself and us!"

But the other criminal rebuked him. "Don't you fear God," he said, "since you are under the same sentence? We are punished justly, for we are getting what our deeds deserve. But this man has done nothing wrong."

Then he said, "Jesus, remember me when you come into your kingdom."

Jesus answered him, "I tell you the truth, today you will be with me in paradise."[1]

—Luke

Precious in the sight of the Lord is the death of his saints.[2]

—The Psalmist

> Well done, good and faithful servant! You have been faithful with a few things; I will put you in charge of many things. Come and share your master's happiness!³
>
> —*The Savior*

A morning at the beach. Waking with the sounds of the ocean: soothing, thrilling. Hearing waves relentlessly pounding the shore and seeing the sun peering over the horizon warms the heart. Problems momentarily fade when confronted with the sea's majesty.

Mountains can also shift the gears of our addictive rituals. Trees, walks through the woods, visits with friends, nice meals, old songs, wide smiles: people and places can capture peaceful spells of removal from the common.

Often, on such trips away, we slowly open eyes after a deep sleep and feel confused. We forget where we are. Expecting the arrangement of procedure, our routine rooms disappear. Windows in new places, smells so unique, noises not normally rolling into ears. Changes shock us but cheer us up. Uncommon clears habitual tension, luring deep breaths and long walks and stars never seen before.

After my trips, though, I love returning home. I know that place. It knows me. Familiar surroundings. Sounds expected. The norm detected. Waking at home satisfies a longing for security and stability.

Christians contend the ultimate wake up call will occur moments after we drift into the inevitable tour out of these bodies. Death. Rapture. If Jesus delays His return each of us will slip into that extreme state of what the Bible calls "sleep." And, if we believe biblical teaching, what a wide-awake, fully-aware nap that will be.

But how can we know for sure we'll stare at glory in a wonderful place? Can the apparent finality of death actually be a door to another more beautiful, more real existence? Scripture deals much with the afterlife. From the scene of Christ's cruel death comes a narrative that gives hope to humans as we march toward our graves.

Jesus suffered the agony of bloody, painful punishment. Crucified between two guilty convicts, a cross clutched a holy, hurting Body. Breaths were hard to absorb, to release. Swallowing wouldn't work right. Bones, muscles, skin: the trapped flesh faced a lock in the zone of realignment. All parts found normal tasks almost impossible. His ears could hear, though. They could receive words spoken by the men on each side. His brain could interpret and understand the noise. Jesus knew the other observers made fun of Him.[4] Those crucified with him also heaped insults on him.

Yet, the behavior of one of the two men soon changed. Drastically. He traded in his cynicism for sensitivity. That decision gave him eternal insurance as Christ assured him they would wake up together in a wonderful place. Let's examine the process of that decision.

A PERSPECTIVE OF YESTERDAY

The dying criminal gained a view of his life's pages as he endured the last chapter while staring at Christ. He decided to respond differently than the man on the other side of Jesus. Their reactions reveal two extremes of perspective. The ways we truly view ourselves rise above the surface during times of crisis. That was such a time for them.

When the curtain began closing on their lives, the man to the left of Jesus and the man to the right of Jesus played the last acts in sharp contrasts. One played the role of pride. The other, humility.

Pride spoke with a curse and a mocking smile: "I'm okay. I'm not really what you'd call a sinner. This is just the way I am. God would never send me to hell. He is supposed to be a loving God and that just wouldn't be fair."

Humility cried with a hope and a dream: "I am a sinner. I was created to live in union with God but my rebellion disrupted the intended harmony. I have rejected my Maker with my attitude and my actions. God owes me nothing. I deserve hell. My only hope stems from God's mercy and the death of Christ."

A correct perspective of life clearly sees the holiness of God and the sinfulness of people. The repentant thief began there. He voted Jesus as innocent, crying out through his pain: "This man has done nothing wrong." He then acknowledged himself as guilty, "We are getting punished justly. We deserve everything that is happening to us." When conclusions blend human wrong with divine righteousness, the results reveal respect for the Just God. The guilty man asked the one on the wrong side of Christ, "Don't you fear God?"

Salvation only grows in the soil of a heart convinced and convicted of sin. First step? Repentance: admission of our complete failure to live perfect lives and a commitment to turn around. The condition is hopeless outside of Christ's redemptive act. Until people begin to grasp how wretched and wicked hearts really are in God's eyes, few will ask for help from the Dying Man in the Middle.

Remember the Prodigal Son? He had to hit bottom before looking up. From the pigpen of his selfishness he realized his failure. He raced home to the arms of a forgiving father.

A pastor explained this in very practical terms. Having frequently taken in troubled teens, he had witnessed the tolls of both pride and humility. Of all the young people he housed during his years of ministry, only three rejected the gospel. To each of the three he said, "You're not low enough yet. You still love sin too much. Go on and let the Devil kick you around. If you're alive when you come to your senses, call me. I'll take you back."

The thief saw himself, and God, correctly. At the end of his life he came to his senses. He gained the proper perspective of what his life had been like. He was ready to move on in the drama of salvation.

A PRAYER FOR TOMORROW

A realization that we deserve punishment begins the journey. Having taken that step, the humble criminal concluded his conversation with the other thief and turned his comments to Jesus. That shows us the next stage coming into focus. The dying man pleaded a request for his future.

Making Reservations: How to Wake in a Wonderful Place

Accurately admitting sin is necessary for moving forward. It would only depress us, though, if the ride ended there. Fortunately, no dead-end, no traps in the mud of sin; the trip continued for that man then. It can continue for us now. There is a way out of the dilemma: soul-searching prayer to the Master.

That dying felon directed his prayer to One who hardly resembled a King of the World. Soldiers watched, possessing regal weaponry and governmental authority. They appeared the most capable candidates of rescue. Instead of begging for mercy from them, however, that man called out to Jesus, One who shared his distress. The request? To deliver him from the agony of that moment, and to direct him in the journey ahead.

To receive assistance, he called upon a Man who had been whipped, ridiculed and humiliated. A Man hanging beside him, dying beside him, suffocating slowly. The man prayed, "Remember me." The words express a hope to be remembered and received for good.[5]

If at such a low state Jesus can assist a desperate man, what can He do for people today from His position of authority? We must, if we hope for His help, offer a prayer as the thief did. And we must offer it with humility and expectancy.

"Jesus, remember me." Notice the simplicity. The specifics. The next statement qualifies the time for the desired recollection: "When you come into your Kingdom." Certainly the penitent thief did not have a full theological grasp of the eschatological ramifications of his request. What did his words show? Death seemed small compared to Eternal Hope.[6]

How often we fail to alert ourselves to the brevity of life. Earthly existence is short. There is much more to life.

Malcolm Forbes flew 600 of his closest friends to North Africa for a $2 million, 70th birthday bash "featuring a 274-man honor guard on horseback and 600 Moroccan belly dancers."[7] Less than a year later he took a nap and never woke up. Jim Henson signed a lucrative deal aligning his lively creations with the magic of Disney, but he did not live to reap the rewards. Such events shout at us: "What shall it profit a man to gain the whole world yet lose his soul?"[8]

I do not know if those men lost their souls. I do not know where they live now, but wherever it is, that is where they will remain. We must learn this: We will exit life on this planet.

What should we do then? Be like the thief who prayed. Today. Offer a prayer for tomorrow.

A PROMISE FOR TODAY

We heard him address the other criminal, the man dying on the opposite side of Jesus. Then we heard words directed to Christ. Now, in the third stage of the process, Jesus offered words. From His place of intense suffering the crucified Christ responded to the thief's request, to his prayer. Jesus promised to help the man beside Him.

Knowing that our eternity is secure gives us great assurance. That confidence soars when we comprehend the present application of God's promise. Tomorrow will be lovely. But today is also in the hand of God!

What great news that gives us. What great news for the thief as he battled for each breath. Hope ruled then, in that moment, as well as in the future. Notice the progression of Christ's encouraging declaration: today...you will...be with Me...in paradise.

Jesus gave him hope for that day, the day of His death. Such hope comes to those who live in Christ's presence in paradise. The promise is not dependent on a criminal's relatives paying and praying him out of the holding pattern of purgatory. There is no mention of a further proving ground to qualify him for entrance into the land of glory. Paradise awaited. Then. Immediately upon his death. How can this astounding fact be true in light of the sinfulness of man we earlier examined?

Jesus told us how:

"For God so loved the world that he gave his one and only Son, that whoever believes in him shall not perish but have eternal life."[9]

God's love makes Christ's statement to the man beside Him possible. So when Jesus told the hurting, humble man they would be together, He spoke with authority. Jesus said it. It was so.

Making Reservations: How to Wake in a Wonderful Place

Eternal salvation equals living together forever in the presence of The Master. That splendid state contrasts severely with eternal damnation which distances souls from God without end. Life forever with God begins at the moment of a conversion experience and enters fullness when the body of flesh gets left behind.[10] Spirits do not separate from Christ then. Not even momentarily. Any power death could boast to do that has, itself, died.[11]

In Acts we read where Stephen preached the message of Jesus. His words made the hearers begin hurling rocks in an attempt to silence him. Jews pummeled him with stones. But because he had gained God's perspective on yesterday, and offered a prayer for tomorrow, he had hope for that day, that moment. As Stephen looked toward the heavens he saw his Hope standing at God's right hand ready to welcome him home.

So it was with the thief who repented. The promise Jesus gave allowed him to breathe his last breath in anticipation of waking from the sleep of death in a wonderful place.

My mind will never forget hitting a last-second shot to win a basketball game when I was ten. I stared at the scoreboard, enthralled by my lucky toss.

At twelve I stood beside Niagara Falls, awed by the powerful beauty of rushing water. My skin felt damp, my mind fell into amazement, my faith found a reminder of a Maker's might.

I placed a kiss on the lifeless face of my mother only moments after her death. I held the hands of my sons only moments after their births.

I have stood on the top of Stone Mountain, holding my boys in my arms. They were small then. The mountain made us seem tall then. Proof of a more powerful, much taller Strength stood above, below and beside us.

Teams I cheer for have won and have lost. I have lived in sickness and in health.

Sunshine, starlight, falling stars, fancy cars, computers, scooters, waves, dolphins, snakes. Two deer approached my breakfast just last week and stared in the window at my eggs, grits, bacon and biscuits.

No experience, though, no matter how stunning, remotely compares to the morning we will wake in the Land of Promise. Tears gone, in that home so far from loneliness, sadness, sin and hurt. And, to see Him. What a joy! No words can, nor ever will, capture the moment that awaits those who wake up in the wonderful place of heaven.

Respond to Christ's Invitation. Live life in anticipation of His reception.

He hopes to see us there.

Make reservations today.

REJOICE that this ministry helps share the Invitation: Founded in 1946, Every Home for Christ has a vision for mobilizing believers to systematically take the Gospel to every family in every home on earth, leaving printed or repeatable gospel messages to help draw the lost to Christ and disciple new believers. More than 300 million homes in 192 nations have been impacted through EHC outreaches, resulting in more than 29 million responses to the Gospel. www.ehc.org

RELEASE your worries by praying, "God, I confess that I deserve to be punished. I thank you for letting Jesus take my place."

RECEIVE Christ's Invitation by asking Him to remember you and forget your failures.

RESPOND by Inviting a friend the way Jesus would. Who will you Invite?

RENEW your mind by reading books by Dick Eastman, Os Guiness, Luis Palau and Henri J.M. Nouwen.

Chapter 20

COME AND HAVE BREAKFAST

Afterward Jesus appeared again to his disciples, by the Sea of Tiberias. It happened this way: Simon Peter, Thomas (called Didymus), Nathanael from Cana in Galilee, the sons of Zebedee, and two other disciples were together. "I'm going out to fish," Simon Peter told them, and they said, "We'll go with you." So they went out and got into the boat, but that night they caught nothing.

Early in the morning, Jesus stood on the shore, but the disciples did not realize that it was Jesus.

He called out to them, "Friends, haven't you any fish?"

"No," they answered.

He said, "Throw your net on the right side of the boat and you will find some." When they did, they were unable to haul the net in because of the large number of fish.

Then the disciple whom Jesus loved said to Peter, "It is the Lord!" As soon as Simon Peter heard him say, "It is the Lord," he wrapped his outer garment around him (for he had taken it off) and jumped into the water.

The other disciples followed in the boat, towing the net full of fish, for they were not far from shore, about a hundred yards. When they landed, they saw a fire of burning coals there with fish on it, and some bread.

Jesus said to them, "Bring some of the fish you have just caught."

Simon Peter climbed aboard and dragged the net ashore. It was full of large fish, 153, but even with so many the net was not torn. Jesus said to them, "Come and have breakfast." None of the disciples dared ask him, "Who are you?" They knew it was the Lord. Jesus came, took the bread and gave it to them, and did the same with the fish. This was now the third time Jesus appeared to his disciples after he was raised from the dead.[1]

—*John, the Beloved Disciple*

> Why spend money on what is not bread,
>   and your labor on what does not satisfy?
> Listen, listen to me, and eat what is good,
>   and your soul will delight in the richest of fare.
> Give ear and come to me;
>   hear me, that your soul may live.
> I will make an everlasting covenant with you,
>   my faithful love promised to David.[2]

—*God,* as recorded by the prophet Isaiah

Over against that terrible word of despair the Lord of history has flung the word, "Emmanuel" (God with us). Morning has broken, and Sunday shouts that Saturday is over; the shackles have been busted and our human condition has been finally and conclusively answered in grace. Grace incarnate, that steps out of the valley of the shadow of death and announces, "I am he that was dead, and behold I am alive forever more."[3]

—*Donald L. Gokee*

Come and Have Breakfast

Nearing the conclusion of His term on earth, Jesus returned to where He began His invitations. Christ initiated His welcomes at the shore of Galilee's Sea, surprisingly greeting some salty fishermen. Those men floated on a three-year mission as their Teacher taught them how to fish for people's souls. This text takes readers back to that beginning point. Finishing where He started, Jesus again noticed men in boats seeking a catch as they fished where they started. What a fitting finale in the last leg of a Savior's journey.

HIGH EXPECTATIONS AND DISAPPOINTING RESULTS: "I'm going out to fish!"

New ventures begin with dreams of grandeur. Full of hope, we leap forward, convinced that end results will match initial desires. Outcomes rarely bring contentment. A new car, purchased with careful scrutiny, turns into a lemon. An ideal relationship fades quickly into another of a long line of failures. A job, that apparent ultimate opportunity, grows too old too quickly. Church services do not thrill the way they once did; the songs sound too old or too new or too many or too few; the pastor's sermons do not move hearts anymore.

The fishermen-turned-disciples felt disillusioned. Jesus never established a Kingdom on earth. At least, not the way His followers expected He would. For all His talk, His walk, and His amazing miracles, they had little practical proof of prophetic phrases Christ linked to Himself. From a crowd of seekers to crucifixion by public opinion. From water into wine to a bloody death. His closest friends dropped into doubt as their dreams dashed. Wasn't Christ supposed to be seated on David's throne? Had their three years of missionary service done anything at all?

Jesus was still alive. But so much had changed. Christ's goal? To place the mantle of ministry upon that group of disciples-turned-fishermen.

Peter, as usual, got things rolling. However his friends felt, he decided to move on. And, as usual, he made his decision public:

"I'm going fishing." Others joined him. They climbed back into a boat to fish, sitting in the setting where Jesus had found them before. With tarnished dreams, they returned to their lives before Christ. They went fishing.

There is nothing, of course, inherently wrong with fishing. Jesus never implied that a return to their nets would equal sin for them. The problem? It was their resignation. Recent events confused them. Jesus spoke words they had trouble understanding. Unsure of Him and themselves, escaping back into their lives before He interrupted looked logical.

The honeymoon had ended. Hard work began. Former ideals looked silly. Too many people give up on their ideals. They chalk up past wishes as naive zeal. The thought of reviewing dreams, rolling up sleeves and laboring to see dream through to reality rarely crosses the minds of moderns who demand instant, and continuous, gratification. That was them. That is us.

During the 1960s, a young generation expressed ideals with enthusiasm. They voiced their longings in protests, music, literature and alternative lifestyles. When they saw how slowly societies change, many became discouraged. Gradually, hippies became yuppies. Joni Mitchell articulated that evolution:

"The 70s were a time in which all of us, having discovered we couldn't change the world, thought that perhaps we could change ourselves. Once we discovered we couldn't change ourselves, we said, 'Well, then, let's make money'."[4]

Watching multitudes dwindle down to just a few discouraged the disciples. It challenged their plan to change the world. Their own cowardice showed during the days of Christ's death. It shook their beliefs. So, like rebels from a generation of change checking their accounts, the friends of Jesus jumped in their boats. Recreation? Escape? Reviving the known? We cannot be sure. We do know that they launched in a boat driven by goals easily attainable and measurable.

Come and Have Breakfast

A LONG NIGHT AND NO FISH: "Friends, haven't you any fish?"

Their night resulted in failure. Had they lost their touch? Their retreat to the safe and familiar surroundings, to the guaranteed success, to escape from a world of surprises and unexpected, imparted further disappointment.

A futile night. Silence. They thought. They remembered. They could mentally hear a Voice that had guided them. They waited for fish, but the animals appeared to not be waiting in return. If they had sought a time of meditation, they got their wish. If they truly hoped to reel high numbers, they failed. An interesting stalemate.

When morning rowed in, Jesus broke the silence. At that point the failing fishermen did not recognize Him. He inquired about their success. They admitted defeat. They had not been ready for a night of fruitless labor. They sure didn't want to broadcast it to a stranger on shore.

Ever have one of those days? Not only does every move backfire, someone else always seems to notice. That is how they must have felt when they told the bad news to an investigator.

A STRANGE SUGGESTION AND STUNNING RESULTS: "Throw your net on the right side."

Our bad day scenarios become worse when the fan on shore opens his mouth instead of just his eyes. When we blow it, egos prefer no one noticing. If they do spy, we would sure hope they keep their mouths shut.

Jesus spoke, possibly making the apparent disaster of the disciples worse. He advised them on a better fishing technique. Remember, those seasoned fishermen had worked through the night. Were they in any mood for an armchair critique? How humiliating.

Jesus told them to try the right side. They proceeded without hesitation. They still did not know the Lord's identity, but maybe eager Peter learned a lesson the first time Jesus directed them to a large catch. Maybe he figured it was worth a shot. So, they lowered their net, following the Stranger's guidelines. That shifted net suddenly filled with fish.

They could not bring in the net because of captured quantity. They didn't need to make up a story about a miracle at sea. What a great illustration of Christ's power, His wisdom, His guidance, His awareness. Utilizing years of education and experience, the efforts of men brought nothing. When their work followed the Word of Jesus, success was immediate.

I often wonder if we have abandoned our ideals and returned to the roles we are most comfortable with. The preaching, healing and traveling may have seemed too much for the less-than-perfect disciples. Fishing posed no problems. They knew technique; they felt confident about their abilities.

Jesus, however, pushes people beyond zones of comfort. He wants His followers in a place where dependency on Him is almost required for the journey to continue.

As He neared the day of ascension, the disciples faced an enormous task. They would find themselves thrust into a new place of responsibility. That is how He wanted it. For them, then. That is how He wants it for us, now.

Those bathed in doubt should not race back to comfort zones of past pleasantries. Christ's fishermen can face the future on knees but face it squarely.

RECOGNIZING A FRIEND AND RACING TO THE SHORE: "It is the Lord!"

To encourage them to fulfill the call, Jesus did not rebuke them. Through an amazing miracle He revealed His power. He opted for showing Himself to them rather than shoving Himself on them. Not volume. Not marketing. Harsh words might have added to their despair. The miracle, reminiscent of the similar episode so long before,[5] taught a lesson no sermon could drive home.

Stare at the result from John's words: "It is the Lord!" His spoken excitement compelled Simon Peter to act. With no desire to conceal his enthusiasm, Peter wrapped his outer garment, dove into the water and traveled the hundred yards like an Olympic swimmer. Peter forgot the fish. His mind was on Jesus. He let the co-workers row in the harvest. He rushed to see his friend. When the boat arrived, Peter reached to drag ashore the net bulging with proof of Christ's powerful promise.

Again, Simon Peter had been caught, lured in, drawn near. Once oblivious to the Face behind the Voice that had asked about their night, Peter then knew the shocking catch paled in comparison to the Person. It really was the Lord! They saw Him. He was there. Alive and with them. Peter's eager plunge showed a longing to be with the Savior. Jesus gladly gave him that opportunity.

AN INVITATION FROM JESUS: "Come and have breakfast."

On the shore they found coals warm and bread ready. They gazed at their Host and knew, for certain, Jesus had Invited them to eat.

He gave them what they thought they needed: a catch of fish. But He gave it on His terms, not theirs. He gave them what their bodies needed: food. He prepared it. He served it. Even more crucial, He gave them what they truly needed in the deepest place of their lives: He gave them Himself.

I marvel at the Invitation to come over for breakfast. He offered not even a small rebuke. A Chef on the verge of clarifying Peter's pastoral commission, He shared Himself. A ministry that began in an encounter with men fishing took its realignment to that familiar bargaining table. The staff felt like giving up, like quitting. Their CEO crashed their pity party and loved them. Out of that context of loving fellowship will emerge the words that indicate the new level of leadership Jesus expected of those wet, hungry men. The Invitations of Jesus ended appropriately; with an Invitation.

All of us are tempted to retreat to safe, secure, more familiar places when initial thrills wane. When we feel too many prayers remain unanswered and too much effort goes unnoticed, we glance around in search of a way out. When pressures of ministry push us to the brink of burn out, we settle for a more comfortable to the flesh, less demanding or challenging role.

The Holy Observer watches us when we sail the boats of resignation. Whether we intend to back off permanently or enjoy a short sabbatical, the Inviter sees. He watches our every move. He knows our every motive. And He loves us.

He also shows up. He glances from the shore as we labor in our efforts to escape the call. He comes not to hammer us with a bitter tirade but to host us at the breakfast table. He meets us right where we are, even in our weakest moments. There He extends that glorious invitation: Come and have breakfast! He does not say come and pay your dues or offer clues or do penance or display a performance. He says, "Let's eat."

You may attempt to anesthetize yourself to your deep hunger. It won't leave. Medicating it through people or pleasure won't fill that place of longing. Promises of earthly satisfaction cover our screens but never materialize. Hollowness haunts throughout eternity in the souls of those who pursue Life merely on an earthly plane. A much better alternative waits. A breakfast at the shore, eating beside the Chef:

> "Turn your eyes upon Jesus.
> Look full in His wonderful face.
> And the things of earth will grow strangely dim,
> In the light of His glory and grace."[6]

Please do not turn down His invitation. At His table waits Life. The Host has chosen those out in the water to ride back, swim back or race back to Him. For Himself. For His mission. For the good of each one, soaking with fresh water.

The adventure began and concluded on the shore with Jesus saying, "Come." He has said it countless times. He says it still. Today. How will you respond?

REJOICE that this ministry helps share the Invitation: You! Yes, you. As you have fallen in love with Him again, that love can be shared to the world.

RELEASE your worries by praying, "God, let's eat!"

RECEIVE Christ's Invitation by celebrating and shouting and rejoicing that He is alive!

RESPOND by Inviting a friend the way Jesus would. Who will you Invite?

RENEW your mind by listening to praise and worship music all week along.

Conclusion

JESUS OF THE INVITATIONS

Read the gospels as a written travelogue. Each verse, story, chapter or account stands alone as an example of the exquisite methodology of sincere evangelism just as each snapshot from a vacation individually reflects a unique experience of life. Unless surveyed as a whole, the completeness escapes and leaves us grasping mere fragments. The totality of a vacation, missed when viewing individual photos, can be seen by observing the album containing all the pictures. Or a video showing the story in motion. Places and people. Good days and bad. Events comprising the entire trip come into focus, accurately portraying a journey that would appear out of balance when only certain pictures were noticed.

This biblical travelogue presents description, like snapshots of a historical person. Knitted together, stories from His life bring into focus a true and astounding picture. More than a portrait of a movement, it is representation of the Man Himself. A Man who loved all the characters of the drama. The lonely? He loved them. The lowly? He loved them. The legalistic? He loved them. Demonstrations of that love differ with each scene, but uniqueness merges with unity; the same pure, profound love shines in every sighting.

Who really is that Great Lover? Is He a rigid, lifeless holy man walking under a halo? Is He a lunatic on a neurotic mission to prove supremacy? Is He a moral mercenary determined to demobilize doubters and sinners by running roughshod along a road of political opportunism? Is He a teacher, one of many who have spoken for God through the ages? Or is He, as He claimed, the Incarnation of God?

Turn to a teacher for a definitive argument regarding Christ's deity. Turn to an apologist for an arsenal of proof-texts to ward off skeptics. Turn toward seeker-friendly styles to find politically correct phrases understood by each age group, race group, doubter group or hopeful group. It's not all here. But, as I learn from so many groups that know so much more, I hope they have taught me to learn from Jesus.

What I've offered is an awareness, just a glimpse, of what the Gospel writers were telling us. These stories have caused me to see Jesus in fresh ways.

During my childhood I learned to accept the doctrine of Christ's deity. That training has served me well and pointed me, I believe, to the greatest truth in all of life. But, over time, spoon-fed truth grows stale. Spiritual vision, once vivid, blurs.

Exploring gospel narratives with wide eyes worked. It dusted off death from my belief system. I have seen a Jesus that shook and shattered. While watching, I have been shaken. I have been shattered. He laughed and cried. Now, I laugh while typing, as tears fall from my eyes.

I am more aware than ever of both my imperfections and His love for me in spite of my frailty. Watching Him with sinners in Matthew's house, seeing Him gaze at the impish Zaccheus while certainly grinning, hearing His powerful words stifle the storm: such scenes moved me despite my familiarity with them. Moments of study offered me the impossible task of laying aside my preconceptions long enough to live through the events unfettered by prematurely drawn conclusions. Along the way, I met Jesus. Again. And He is very real, very alive.

Those who have never set foot onto the path of Jesus lack much. It would be far too simplistic to imply that following Him cures all ills, or renders one continually happy. It could be equally untrue and entirely unfair to pretend that uniting our lives with His makes little difference. Deciding to investigate the "who" question of Jesus can start you down the road where the "what," "why," and "how" questions of life become answered in deep, dynamic ways.

If you were, like I was, born and bred in the briar patch of Christianity, praise God. Thank your parents and your pastors and the martyrs and the saints. But beware. The eternal truths you've come to so readily accept may have grown musty and rusty. Familiarity with theology can make us more religious than Christian. Unless Christ comes with The Story.

Read and reread the Invitations of Jesus. Look earnestly for the real Savior. Refuse to settle for what you have heard. Do not reject tradition, but do not attempt to confine Christ in a cage of the common. Training may be accurate, but we desperately need the jolt a new look at Jesus can bring.

Annie Dillard, in The Living, articulates a caution: "No child on earth was ever meant to be ordinary, and you can see it in them, and they know it, too, but then the times get to them, and they wear out their brains learning what folks expect, and spend their strength trying to rise over those same folks."

Don't we notice how eager efforts of maturity rob us of childlike earnestness? Our removal of crawling and crying has also robbed our romance. May the thirst for Milk return. May the thrill of Joy refill. May the theory never rob the reformation of faith in Father, Son and Holy Spirit.

I read The Sacred Romance and nod an "amen," before filling my time with people, places and things in a life too busy for the Time Maker. I read George Barna's stats of church hopping, doctrinal indifference, and troubling trends, and I undergo an inner disturbance. I pray the Prayer of Jabez, but I also cry with David in his Psalms of painful poetic prayers, repeat Paul's rebukes in his epistles, and find myself sleeping with disciples while a Sacrifice intercedes. I worry.

But I also see a 10/40 Window showing new colors with blood-red truth and clear, white reception. I observe missions groups partnering instead of competing, denominations learning from each other rather than rebuking doctrinal diversity, Americans learning Christian beliefs from fresh believers around the globe, and many churches paying attention to God by giving Him a chance to be The Audience. I rejoice.

We have heard so often that He is the way, the truth and the life. We accept such statements religiously. We also allow them to remain removed from reality. New Testament stories, when read or heard with anticipation, transform trite quotes into a wind that blows away religious routines. When all our attempts at coming to God appear blocked, we can then see Him as The Way, not just merely a way among many. When handicapped by lies from within and deception from without, He bursts onto the scene as The Truth, no longer only a true character in history. When the stench of death seeps from the pores of relational contacts and religious concerns, He brings Life, not life, as He offers the Gift of Himself.

God incarnate. Not a choice among choices. The Choice. Either come through Jesus or abandon all hope of finding God. That summarizes a belief system of Christianity.

Skeptics ridicule these exclusive claims without stopping their ranting long enough to understand the depths Jesus traveled to make those claims inclusive. Only through Jesus? Yes. But all may come. He pockets no checklist of virtuous requirements to prohibit the entrance of unqualified applicants. He accepts the ones entering seriously. He holds the key to unlock prisons in which they find themselves jailed. He copies and pastes Himself through a Spirit Holy, beaming Hope to those open for His Help.

May we refuse to think lightly of Jesus. May we refrain from a closeness to Him that merely leaves us callous to His majesty. By adjusting our Christology we will surely attend our need for Him in the arena of daily life. We need, individually and congregationally and globally, to once again find Jesus.

Let our times of pretending to bow by the throne be crushed. Let us settle for the True Jesus. Nothing less.

Find Him in His earthiness and His heavenliness. By doing so He will touch the earth of our lives with the Heaven of His own. And isn't that what Life is all about?

NOTES

Chapter 1: A Simple Invitation
1. John 1:35-42. (Unless otherwise indicated, all Scripture quotations are taken from the New International Version of the Bible.) (Note: Throughout this study I will assume the traditional position regarding authorship of biblical accounts.)
2. Robert E. Coleman, *The Master Plan of Evangelism* (Old Tappan, N.J.: Fleming H. Revell, 1963), 21.
3. E.M. Bounds, *Power Through Prayer* (Grand Rapids: Baker Book House, 1977), 5.
4. Gayle D. Erwin, *The Jesus Style* (Waco, Texas: Word Books, 1983), 19.
5. Isaiah 53:2.
6. Luke 2:7.
7. Matthew 5:8.
8. Bill Hull, *Jesus Christ Disciple-Maker* (Colorado Springs: NavPress, 1984), 18.
9. Hull, 18.
10. *Hebrew-Greek Key Study Bible, New Testament*, ed. Spiros Zodhiates (Chattanooga, TN: AMG Publishers, 1984), 435.
11. J.I. Packer, *Knowing God* (Downers Grove, Illinois: InterVarsity Press, 1973), 196.
12. Mark 3:14.

13. LeRoy Eims, *The Lost Art of Disciplemaking* (Grand Rapids: Zondervan/Colorado Springs: NavPress, 1978), 67.
14. R.V.G. Tasker, *The Gospel According to St. John*, Tyndale New Testament Commentaries (Grand Rapids: Wm. B. Eerdmans, 1960), 52.
15. Coleman, 38.
16.. Erwin, 69.
17. 2 Corinthians 7:6.
18. Hebrews 6:19.
19. John 14:6.
20. 1 John 1:9.
21. Psalm 112:7.
22. 2 Corinthians 2:14.
23. Tasker, 52.
24. Acts 4:20.
25. Coleman, 24.
26. Hull, 23.

Chapter 2: Following the Leader
1. John 1:43-50.
2. C.S. Lewis, *The Inspirational Writings of C.S. Lewis*, "The Business of Heaven" (New York: Inspirational Press, 1984), 311.
3. John Wimber, *Power Evangelism* (San Francisco: Harper & Row, 1986), xvii.
4. John 6:44.
5. A.W. Tozer, *The Pursuit of God* (Christian Publications, Inc., 1948), 11.
6. John 1:41.
7. R.V.G. Tasker, *The Gospel According to St. John*, Tyndale New Testament Commentaries (Grand Rapids: Wm. B. Eerdmans, 1960), 53.
8. John 1:50.
9. Elmer Town, *Winning the Winnable* (Lynchburg, Virginia: Church Growth Institute, 1987), 6.
10. Joe Aldrich, *Life-Style Evangelism* (Portland, Oregon: Multnomah Press, 1981), 15, 16.

Notes

Chapter 3: Gone Fishin'
1. Matthew 4:18-22.
2. Genesis 3:9.
3. Henri J.M. Nouwen, *Clowning In Rome* (Garden City, N.Y.: Image Books, 1979), 21.
4. W. Phillip Keller, *Rabboni* (Old Tappan, N.J.: Fleming H. Revell, 1977), 84.
5. Keller, 17.
6. *Key Study Bible*, 504.
7. Luke 5:10b.

Chapter 4: Excuses, Excuses
1. Matthew 8:18-22.
2. Art Reynolds, "Jesus Is Just Alright With Me," copyright 1969 & 1972, Alexis Music 1 YOLK Music.
3. Richard M. Sherman, "Robert B. Sherman," Spoonful of Sugar, copyright 1963, Wonderland Music.
4. F.F. Bruce, *The Hard Sayings of Jesus* (Downers Grove, Illinois: InterVarsity Press, 1983). 15.
5. R.C.H. Lenski, T*he Interpretation of St. Luke's Gospel* (Minneapolis, Minnesota: Augsburg Publishing House, 1961), 559.
6. Lenski, 561.
7. Suzanne de Dietrich, *The Layman's Bible Commentary: Matthew* (Richmond, Virginia: John Knox Press, 1961), 54.
8. Luke 9:62.
9. Lenski, 563.
10. Matthew 6:33.
11. Philippians 4:19.
12. Keith Green, "Pledge My Head To Heaven," copyright 1980, Birdwing Music/Cherry Lane Music Publishing Co., Inc.
13. Bruce, 16.

Chapter 5: A Familiar Face in a Frightening Place
1. Luke 8:22-25.
2. Joshua 1:5, 9.
3. John 14:25-27.

4. 1 John 4:18.
5. Hebrews 13:8.
6. Luke 8:23.
7. Frederick Buechner, *Peculiar Treasures* (San Francisco: Harper & Row, 1979), 63.
8. Hebrews 7-8.
9. Hebrews 13:5.
10. 2 Corinthians 5:7.
11. Daniel 3:25.
12. Genesis 45:5.
13. Romans 12:2.
14. Lance DeMers, "I Am," copyright 1978, Dimension Music.
15. Romans 8:28.

Chapter 6: A Friend To the Friendless
1. Matthew 9:9-13.
2. R.V.G. Tasker, *Tyndale New Testament Commentaries: The Gospel According to St. Matthew* (Grand Rapids: Wm. B. Eerdmans, 1961), 98.
3. Steven R. Mosley, *A Tale of Three Virtues* (Sisters, Oregon: Questar Publishers, Inc., 1989), 19.
4. Haddon Robinson, "Good Guys, Bad Guys and Us Guys" (Haddon Robinson, 1990), Preaching Today, Tape #80.
5. Matthew 10:3 (cf. Mark 3:18; Luke 6:15).
6. Tasker, 106.
7. Haddon Robinson, *Foreword: Life-Style Evangelism,* Joseph C. Aldrich (Portland, Oregon: Multonomah Press, 1981), 11.
8. Luke 19:10.
9. Philippians 2:7.
10. Robinson, "Good Guys, Bad Guys and Us Guys."
11. John Fischer, *Real Christians Don't Dance* (Minneapolis: Bethany House Publisher, 1988), 124 & 125.
12. Luke 5:28.
13. Frederick Buechner, *The Magnificent Defeat* (New York: Harper & Row, 1966), 99.
14. Matthew 13:31-33.
15. 2 Corinthians 5:18.

16. Matthew 9:13.
17. George W. Peters, *A Theology of Church Growth* (Grand Rapids: Zondervan Publishing House, 1981), 97.
18. Eugene Kennedy, *The Choice To Be Human* (Garden City, New York: Doubleday & Co., 1985), 92.

Chapter 7: Life After Death
1. Mark 5:35-43.
2. Calvin Miller, *The Singer* (Downer's Grove: InterVarsity Press, 1975), 139.
3. Augustine.
4. Matthew 28:20b.
5. Mark 5:34.
6. Hebrews 11:1.
7. Luke 8:55.
8. Alan Cole, *Tyndale New Testament Commentaries: The Gospel According to St. Mark* (Grand Rapids: Wm. B. Eerdmans, 1961), 130.
9. Mark 5:43.
10. Hebrews 13:5.
11. John 20:29.
12. Isaiah 55:8; 1 Corinthians 13:12.
13. John 11:25.
14. Luke 10:20.

Chapter 8: Coming To Christ For the Rest of Your Life
1. Matthew 11:28-30.
2. Rollo May, quoted in *Growing Strong In The Seasons of Life*, Charles R. Swindoll (Portland: Multnomah Press, 1983), 216.
3. David A. Seamonds, *Healing of Memories* (Wheaton, Illinois: Victor Books, 1985), 101.
4. Walter Bauer, tr. William F. Arndt and F. Wilbur Gingrich, *A Greek-English Lexicon of the New Testament* (Chicago: University of Chicago Press, 1958), 698.
5. Philippians 2:5-8.
6. Acts 5:10.
7. Luke 11:46.

8. Bauer, Arndt, Gingrich, 886.
9. Bauer, Arndt, Gingrich, 443.
10. John 4:6.
11. Bauer, Arndt, Gingrich, 865.
12. Matthew 11:28, King James Version.
13. Swindoll, 136.
14. Philippians 4:7.
15. Lawrence J. Crabb, Jr., *Effective Biblical Counseling* (Grand Rapids: Zondervan, 1977), 20.
16. Swindoll, 136 & 137.

Chapter 9: Thirsty For Love
1. John 4:4-26.
2. Lawrence J. Crabb, Jr., *Understanding People* (Grand Rapids: Zondervan, 1987), 120.
3. Rebecca Manley Pippert, *Hope Has Its Reasons* (San Francisco: Harper & Row, 1989), 16.
4. Luke 5:31.
5. Luke 15:2.
6. 1 Corinthians 9:19-23.
7. Proverbs 25:11.
8. Duncan Buchanan, *The Counseling of Jesus* (Downers Grove, Illinois: InterVarsity Press, 1985), 34.
9. 2 Timothy 1:8, Romans 1:16.
10. John 4:28.

Chapter 10: Missing The Boat
1. Matthew 14:22-36.
2. Malcolm Smith, *Spiritual Burnout* (Tulsa: Honor Books, 1988), 119.
3. George Mueller.
4. Albert Barnes, *Notes on the New Testament: Matthew & Mark* (Grand Rapids: Baker Book House, 1949), 156.
5. R.C. Trench, *Notes on the Miracles of Our Lord* (Grand Rapids: Baker Book House, 1949), 175.
6. Isaiah 50:10, paraphrased.
7. Trench, 174.

8. Matthew 14:27b.
9. Ada R. Habershon, *The Study of the Miracles* (Grand Rapids: Kregel Publications, 1957), 130.
10. John Pollock, *The Master* (Wheaton: Victor Books, 1985), 97.
11. Barnes, 156.
12. *Hebrew-Greek Key Study Bible, New Testament*, ed. Spiros Zodhiates (Chattanooga, Tennessee: AMG Publishers, 1985), 472.
13. Richard J. Foster, *Celebration of Discipline*, Revised Edition (San Francisco: Harper & Row, 1978, 1988), 108 & 109.
14. Charles R. Swindoll, *Growing Strong In The Season of Life* (Portland: Multnomah Press, 1983), 174.
15. Galatians 2:20.

Chapter 11: Awards, Autographs and A Kid in the Middle
1. Matthew 18:1-4.
2. John White, *The Golden Cow* (Downers Grove: InterVarsity Press, 1979), 94.
3. Anthony Campolo, Jr., *The Power Delusion* (Wheaton: Victor Books, 1983), 45.
4. Matthew 20:20, 21.
5. James 4:1-3.
6. James 4:10.
7. Tasker, 175.
8. John 3:30.
9. 2 Corinthians 12:8-10.
10. Philippians 2:6-8.
11. John 13:1-17.
12. Luke 22:25-27.
13. Mark 8:35.
14. Matthew 13:31-32.

Chapter 12: Leaving The Back Door Open
1. Matthew 19:16-30.
2. Calvin Miller, *The Singer* (Downers Grove: InterVarsity, 1975), 43.

3. John Donne, "Ravished By God," *The John Donne Treasury* (Wheaton: Victor Books, 1978), 53.
4. Bob Bennett, "Matters of the Heart," copyright 1982, Priority Music/CBS Inc.
5. Bruce, 176.
6. Matthew 18:12-14.
7. Pippert, 47.
8. Bob Mumford, sermon: "The Pearl Trader's Society," 1990.
9. For a thorough examination of this, see Becky Pippert's *Hope Has Its Reasons*. She analyzes this thought brilliantly and in detail.

Chapter 13: No Sudden Moves, Please
1. Luke 14:25-35.
2. John White, *Daring to Draw Near* (Downers Grove: InterVarsity Press, 1977), 150.
3. Mike Yaconelli, *Tough Faith* (Elgin, Illinois: David C. Cook, 1976), 63.
4. Bruce, 119 & 120.
5. Philippians 3:8.
6. Bruce, 151.
7. Galatians 5:24.
8. Revelation 3:20.
9. Bauer, Arndt, Gingrich, 100.
10. Robert Johnson, "Heavenly Gifts," *The Wall Street Journal*, December 11, 1990.
11. 1 Corinthians 10:24.
12. Pippert, 161.
13. Bruce, 37.

Chapter 14: Beggars Can Be Chosen
1. Mark 10:46-52.
2. Andrew Murray, *With Christ In The School of Prayer* (Whitaker House, 1981), 64.
3. Bob Bennett, "Beggar," copyright 1982, Priority Music/CBS Songs.
4. Murray, 64.

5. Frederick Buechner, *Wishful Thinking* (New York: Harper & Row, 1973), 70 & 71.
6. Cole, 173.
7. Bill Hybels, *Who You Are When No One's Looking* (Downers Grove: InterVarsityPress, 1987), 47.
8. Suzanne de Dietrich, 107.
9. Buechner, *Wishful Thinking*, 71.

Chapter 15: A Small Man With A Tall Plan
1. Luke 19:1-10.
2. Chuck Colson.
3. Jim Wallis, *The Call To Conversion* (San Francisco: Harper & Row, 1981), 4.
4. Frederick Buechner, *Peculiar Treasures* (San Francisco: Harper & Row, 1979), 180.
5. Luke 19:10.
6. Read the major and minor Old Testament prophets, the gospels and Acts to see the priority of the message of repentance.
7. Wallis, 4.
8. Buechner, *Peculiar Treasurers*, 180.
9. Buchanan, 89.

Chapter 16: Dressed For Success
1. Matthew 22:1-14.
2. Dr. John H. Gerstner, "Jesus and Hell," Ligonier Ministries: TABLETALK (Walk Thru The Bible Ministries, Inc., 1990), Volume 14, Number 7, July 1990, 8.
3. Matthew 7:22 & 23.
4. Matthew 21:45 & 46.
5. Luke 14:16-24.
6. *The Pulpit Commentary, St. Matthew, Vol. II*, (New York: Funk & Wagnalls Company), 358.
7. Luke 13:27 & 28.
8. Matthew 5:22, 29, 30; 10:28; 18:9; 23:33; Luke 16:23.
9. Jonathan Edwards, "Sinners In the Hands of An Angry God."

Chapter 17: Does Anybody Really Know What Time It Is?
1. Matthew 25:1-13.
2. Bob Dylan, "Slow Train," copyright 1979, Special Rider Music.
3. Edgar Whisenant, *88 Reasons Why The Rapture Will Be In 1988* (Nashville: World Bible Society, 1987).
4. Robert Lamm, "Does Anybody Really Know What Time It Is?," copyright 1972, Columbia/CBS Records/Chicago Music.
5. Matthew 24:3.
6. Matthew 25:6b.
7. Tasker, 233.
8. Revelation 16:15; 1 Thessalonians 5:2.
9. 1 Thessalonians 5:4.
10. 1 Thessalonians 5:4-11.
11. Bauer, Arndt, Gingrich, 539.
12. Philippians 2:13.
13. 1 Thessalonians 5:9, paraphrased.
14. Romans 14:1, 19; 15:1, 2, 7.
15. Bruce, 233 & 235.
16. Romans 11:22.
17. Revelation 9:6b.
18. Luke 12:40.
19. Matthew 24:44, 25:13.
20. Revelation 19:15.

Chapter 18: Spending the Night
1. Matthew 26:36-45.
2. Miller, 87.
3. Poster, 33.

Chapter 19: How To Wake Up In A Wonderful Place
1. Luke 23:39-43.
2. Psalm 116:15.
3. Matthew 25:21.
4. Mark 15:32.

5. Leon Morris, *Tyndale New Testament Commentaries: The Gospel According To St. Luke* (Grand Rapids: William B. Eerdmans, 1974), 328.
6. Morris, 329.
7. Chuck Colson, "From Acquisition To Altruism: The Empty Pursuit," *Jubilee*, May 1990 Prison Fellowship, 7.
8. Mark 8:36, paraphrased.
9. John 3:16.
10. 2 Corinthians 5:8.
11. Philippians 1:23.

Chapter 20: Come and Have Breakfast
1. John 21:1-4.
2. Isaiah 55:2, 3.
3. Donald L. Gokee, *It's A Love-Haunted World* (Lima, Ohio: C.S.S. Publishing Co, Inc., 1985), 98.
4. Joni Mitchell in "Waking Up From the California Dream," *The New York Times*, August 6, 1989.
5. Luke 5:1-11.
6. Helen H. Lemmel, "Turn Your Eyes Upon Jesus," 1922.

Printed in the United States
1052500003B/214